THE COMPLETE CASES
OF JOHNNY CASS

THE COMPLETE CASES OF

JOHNNY CASS™

ROGER D. TORREY

INTRODUCTION BY

WILL MURRAY

ILLUSTRATIONS BY

JOHN FLEMING GOULD

POPULAR PUBLICATIONS • 2022

TABLE OF CONTENTS

INTRODUCTION
BY WILL MURRAY

I N THE 21st Century, Roger Denzel Torrey is remembered as a prolific practitioner of the Hard-Boiled School of detective writing, one who wrote heavily for the Speed line of pulp magazines in the 1940s. The Speed titles had been the salacious Spicy chain and its magazines, such as *Private Detective Stories* and *Speed Detective*, were carrying on the hardboiled private eye tradition after other publishers and writers had moved on to telling a different kind of tale as the 1940s called for a fresh approach to the genre.

As such, Torrey's reputation today is that of a hack.

But that was not how his contemporaries saw him, especially during the early 1930s when he was a regular contributor to the respected pages of *Black Mask*, the wellspring of the Hard-Boiled School.

"Forrest Rosaire and Roger Torrey are, to my mind, two of the most promising writers in the field of crime fiction since Dashiell Hammett." *Black Mask* regular James H.S. Moynahan wrote those words in 1936.

That statement alone is a testament to the type of writer Torrey was. More to the point, Torrey served no pulp apprenticeship before cracking the coveted *Black Mask* market. One did not usually break into print through *Black Mask*, especially under the editorship of Captain Joseph T.

Shaw. *Black Mask* was considered the premier magazine in its genre. This is the periodical that launched the careers of Dashiell Hammett and Raymond Chandler. To place a story in its pages made you one of the legendary *Black Mask* boys. The cream of the crop. The top of the heap. Along with Paul Cain, Erle Stanley Gardner, Frederick Nebel, and others.

According to his own account, Torrey's first fiction submission was rejected, but Joe Shaw took his second, "Police Business," late in 1932. For the next half-dozen years, Torrey was a frequent contributor to *Black Mask,* appearing in the majority of its monthly issues. That took effort. Cap Shaw was a demanding editor, and often sent a submission back for revision. Immediately after breaking in with the January, 1933 issue, Roger Torrey became a *Black Mask* fixture. Some writers, such as Raymond Chandler, did exactly that and then moved on to the bestseller lists and eventually Hollywood.

Not Roger Torrey. His career began with Mount Kilimanjaro of pulp peaks, maintained its position for a fair number of years but soon went into a gradual and then accelerating decline.

During the 1930s, and even into the 1940s, after he'd begun wordsmithing for the Speed magazines, Roger Torrey was considered by his fellow writers as only a notch or two beneath Dashiell Hammett and Cornell Woolrich. That was rarefied atmosphere indeed.

Why was this so?

It was simple. Torrey wrote tough. And the kind of toughness he communicated through his stories was not the artificial one of pulpsters who aped Hammett or even Carroll John Daly, but the kind of authentic stuff a writer could pen only if his life experiences had exposed him to the seamier side of life.

Black Mask contributor James H.S. Moynahan praised Torrey's work in 1936:

> Torrey's excellence lies in the very simplicity of his authen-
> ticity. He knows how men act when they are angry or frightened
> and he makes them act that way. For example: Torrey knows
> that a pistol is a terrifying thing, and his hero is not ashamed to
> admit that he finds it so. Such honesty in popular fiction is
> almost unheard of. But it pays Mr. Torrey handsome dividends
> in making his yarns convincing.
>
> Like Dashiell Hammett, Torrey knows mugs from association
> with them: he knows, he doesn't just guess. And it is in *setting
> down the psychology of the mug where it differs from the ordinary
> citizen's* that Torrey is so simply true that you recognize the
> touch at once as beyond artifice.

For that reason and others, Steve Fisher called him "probably one of the finest writers *Black Mask* ever had."

Born in Bay City, Michigan in 1901, Roger Torrey had lived an ordinary life until Prohibition came along. His stepfather owned a number of theaters in Klamath Falls, Oregon, during the silent film era. These establishments also put on stage plays and vaudeville performances. Torrey learned to play the piano to accompany silent films and for a number of years he followed this career, playing piano and organ in cities up and down the West Coast, as well as in Tulsa, Oklahoma and Kansas City, Missouri.

Torrey also played piano in various speakeasies, pool halls and card rooms, and conceivably bordellos, and this brought him into contact with the seedy side of the Roaring Twenties. Apparently, young Torrey was quite comfortable doing this work. As a compulsive gambler in his younger years, he was in his element.

Additionally, Torrey was a heavy drinker. Consequently, he felt the need to move on frequently. No doubt he was often fired. Newspaper accounts tell of his repeated drink driving misadventures. Possibly the young honky tonk musician was compelled to escape accumulating debts. Perhaps he was also at times just one step at the head of the law. You didn't work in speakeasies without rubbing shoulders with the various inhabitants of the Underworld, the mugs, yeggs and cops alike, and perhaps coming into conflict with one side of the other of the crime-and-punishment dynamic of the bootlegger era. Torrey spent a lot of time in Chiloquin, an Oregon boom town infamous as the "little Chicago," where he played barrelhouse piano in its speakeasies and managed the Chiloquin Theater for a time circa 1928.

His musical skills apparently insured there was always a town or city that would welcome his services. But nothing is forever. When talkies came in at the tail end of the 1920s, silent films lost their popular appeal, and work dried up completely.

Briefly, Torrey and his wife Edna set up a confectionery store next to his father's main theater in Klamath, Oregon. This does not seem to have worked out. Neither did the marriage. The Stock Market crash of October, 1929 no doubt played a role in Torrey's declining and increasingly uncertain fortunes.

It was at this point that Torrey wrote his first stories and discovered he could make a living at the typewriter. In that way, he was exactly like Raymond Chandler, who also turned to *Black Mask* after his cushy oil-company executive position evaporated with the stock market. Torrey beat Chandler into print by eleven months.

Unfortunately, Torrey couldn't stay out of trouble. Early in 1933, flush with *Black Mask* money, he sailed confidently into one of the most disreputable establishments in Klamath Falls, a vice den called the Palm Hotel, and either was robbed or swindled out of it. The police were called in. Torrey complained. He was arrested on drunk and disorderly charges, and fined. The hotel owner was deported back to France. Newspapers don't report whether Torrey got any of his money back. It's doubtful that he did.

Torrey got a lucky break when he came into contact with agent Lurton Blassingame. Up until this time, he had been strictly a creature of *Black Mask*. Blassingame pointed him toward other markets, chiefly Popular Publications' *Dime Detective Magazine*, which was *Black Mask's* main rival and paid competitively.

A year after breaking in, Torrey found himself filling constant orders for *Black Mask* and *Dime Detective,* and then branching out into rival magazines ranging from *Detective Fiction Weekly* to *Ten Detective Aces.* His name became a familiar one on top pulp covers and contents pages. Torrey's work was in demand. He wrote Blassingame that for August, 1938, he made almost as much pulp money as he usually earned in a calendar year prior to selling through the agent.

Torrey was not only well regarded due to the authenticity of his characters and the smoky barroom world in which he placed them, but as an avid hunter, he knew firearms intimately. This knowledge also set him head and shoulders above the average pulp writer, who may or may not ever have fired a weapon. It has been said a Roger Torrey story was notable for the way he accurately described the action and sound of whatever guns were going off in a scene. Because he knew.

He also had the correct touch with regard to humor. When Torrey's stories called for it, his narration and dialogue had exactly the correct style of world-weary, cynical humor that was a trademark of 1930s detective fiction, as exemplified by Humphrey Bogart in his cinematic portrayals of characters on either side of the law.

It's not surprising that filling editorial orders gave Torrey plenty of time leisure time in which to drink, particularly after Prohibition was repealed in 1933. His drinking, if anything, accelerated. When he hadn't the money for the real stuff, Torrey reportedly resorted to drinking Lilac Vegetal aftershave lotion, whose alcohol content satisfied his urges.

One of Torrey's drinking buddies later claimed that his real name was Torres. But in fact, the Torrey family were Irish on both sides, and more often than not, his protagonists were Irish-Americans. But such were the myths that arose around such semi-literary figures. Was this a white lie that Torrey told? Or simply someone's flawed memory of something overheard? It's unknown. But Torrey was not above exaggerating his background. Steve Fisher recalled him as a former lumberjack. But the truth was that Torrey merely kept the books for a sawmill. No outdoorsy toppler of mighty trees, only a desk-bound accountant. This was only one of the many short-term jobs Torrey was forced to take in his knockabout life before he discovered the typewriter could make him a comfortable living. To his credit, during World War I, Torrey served a year with the Royal Canadian Rifles after the U.S. Army rejected the 17-year-old as too young. He lied about his age and citizenship.

And his career expanded, Torrey became friendly with many writers and entertainers on both coasts. The tale was told that Torrey once tried to borrow fifteen dollars from Dashiell Hammett, and Hammett, no doubt wisely, refused. An angry Torrey, along with accomplice Carroll John Daly, did not take the refusal calmly.

"They were drunk and he wouldn't give it to them," recalled Daly's daughter. "So they broke his plate-glass window."

Such behavior, as well as frequent demands for advances from editors on the promise of a finished story in the future, as well as pay-rate disputes, caused some editors to turn their backs on him. Frank Gruber recalled that one editor actually counted the words in a Torrey manuscript rather than pay on the basis of the author's estimated word count, which led to an undercount. According to Gruber, Torrey "blew his top." Every penny counted when one was paid by the number of pennies per word. Times stayed tough, even as the Great Depression started to lift.

Despite being a rising star only three years into the game, by 1936, Torrey's byline began appearing in some of the trashier, lower-paying pulps, such as *Star Detective Magazine*, *True Gang Life*, and *Detective and Murder Mysteries*. Some of these magazines paid on publication, if at all.

He dropped out of *Dime Detective* after contributing only six stories, despite the fact that the magazine liked to lure *Black Mask* contributors into its pages with offers of a higher word rate. What happened? No one today knows. But only three stories in, with "A Death in the Family," his protagonist, Los Angeles private eye Johnny Cass, was renamed Johnny Carr. Probably because John Lawrence's Cass Blue had begun appearing regularly in the same pages and the editors didn't want their readers confused by two characters with somewhat similar names.

Perhaps that change was enough to tick off the author, and he took his talents elsewhere. Torrey had a reputation for being hot tempered. Steve Fisher recalled that when *Ten Detective Aces* rejected one of Torrey's submissions, which had also been bounced by *Black Mask*, the author angrily simply tore up the manuscript and tossed it into the editor's waste basket. This, despite the fact of Torrey never made carbons of his stories.

When *Black Mask's* Joe Shaw was let go in September, 1936, and word rates reportedly cut, Torrey did not abandon the market as many of his contemporaries had. But he found selling to the new editor increasingly difficult.

"Fanny Ellsworth took over," recalled Steve Fisher, "and other authors began to appear on the coveted contents page: upstarts, Johnny-come-latelys, Frank Gruber, Cornell Woolrich and Steve Fisher among them."

New blood writing in this new style meant stiffer competition to a writer not accustomed to having to compete. After years of appearing in almost every issue of *Black Mask,* the Torrey byline was seen less often. In 1940, the year Popular Publications took over the title and installed Ken White, Jr., as editor, Roger Torrey struggled to sell to his first and foremost market. His last *Black Mask* story ran in 1942, nearly ten years after making his first sale.

He found some shreds of dignity in selling to Munsey's *Detective Fiction Weekly* and *Street & Smith's Detective Story Magazine,* whose editor, Daisy Bacon, held his work up as a prime example of the "modern" detective tale, observing "I always thought that he and Jonathan Latimer had a good old-fashioned down-to-earth touch with sex that a good many of the other tough writers lacked."

Cryptically, Bacon also noted that "He always seem to be living one of his own stories." Yet she accepted his work infrequently. That wasn't enough to support him.

Thus, Torrey found himself slumming for *Spicy Detective Stories, Private Detective Stories, Hollywood Detective,* and *Speed Detective* after *Black Mask* wouldn't have him anymore. He adopted two pen names, John Ryan and Sam Drake, used when he wrote his first-person stories of detectives by those names.

During the latter 1930s, Torrey had relocated to New York City to be closer to editorial offices. At a meeting of the American Fiction Guild, he connected with another writer, Helen Ahern, who wrote for the romance pulps. The two of them shacked up, living off their yarn-spinning and drank prodigiously. They appeared to be made for one another. He nicknamed Helen "Mommy."

In a 1972 *Armchair Detective* memoir, Steve Fisher recalled the couple vividly:

> They both liked to drink, but liquor is expensive, so Roger made a rule. His writing table was on one side of the room, her desk on the other. Each would sit down in front of his/her typewriter, their backs to one another, and the one to finish his/her story first could then have a drink. The other would have to wait until her story was completed. I say "her" in this case because Helen couldn't write as fast as Roger, and he, that bastard, would sit there on the floor boozing it up and taunting poor "Mommy."
>
> Roger Torrey was drinking too much, and a doctor told him his liver was about gone and to stop. He did, for a month, then with a "what the hell" attitude ordered a case of Scotch sent up to the room.
>
> I used to write until one in the morning, or after, and so did he; and then, too often, really, I'd meet him at a bar in New York. Helen would of course be along. We'd drink until closing time

at 4 a.m., then sometimes take a cab through the Holland tunnel to New Jersey where the bars remained open until 6.

It was after one such night that I accompanied him and Helen back to that untidy hotel room and promptly flaked out on the divan. When I woke up there were two or three bellboys in the room carrying things out. I asked what the hell was going on.

"We've decided to move to Florida," Helen said.

Helen owned a battered car and Roger had a few dollars in his pocket.

The car broke down in Delaware, and they wired me for twenty-five dollars.

I sent it.

This occurred in 1942. Temporarily residing in Virginia Beach, they tied the knot, becoming husband and wife. Fisher continued:

Roger and Helen reached Florida all right, and sending their stories to New York, earned enough to live on—and booze on. They were happy, Helen told me. Perhaps Roger Torrey's first and only happiness.

During the war years, they called Fort Lauderdale home. Other than the odd arrest for public intoxication, they lived quietly with their two dogs and a cat. One Setter Schnauzer was called Trojan, no doubt named after the pulp publishing house that kept them in gin-soaked comfort.

Increasingly, Torrey's magazine tales are laid in Florida and adjoining states. This was a common practice among pulp scribes. To obtain fresh material and locales, they moved often, and their work reflected this fact of life.

One day in January 1946, his liver finally failed and Roger Torrey died.

After returning to New York City, Helen Torrey told the story to Steve Fisher, who remembered it this way:

> Then one afternoon he felt poorly and lay down on a couch and asked if she'd make him some tea. Helen brought the tea. Roger sipped it, thanking her, then rested his head on the pillow.
>
> "Hold my hand, Mommy, because I'm going to die."
>
> She held his hand and Roger Torrey closed his eyes for the last time.

Roger Torrey was only 45 years old. Although he had sold literally hundreds of stories over the previous thirteen years, Torrey had produced only one book, *Forty-Two Weeks of Murder.* All the rest were in the pulps, which in that era were considered as disposable as yesterday's newspapers.

Yet Torrey's "Clean Sweep" was reprinted in Joe Shaw's hardcover *Hard-Boiled Omnibus* several months after he died.

In his introduction, Joe Shaw wrote this:

> Roger Torrey stands high in the list of those who contributed most to *Black Mask's* distinctive style. He's writing was hard and it was "brittle." His characters were hard and tough and so convincing as only to have been drawn from actual observations and experience. Yet, tough as they were, Roger always found some good beneath. The cause might be unlawful and even venal, but somewhere along the line or in the payoff, that good would come out in a way of loyalty or sense of decency. And perhaps it was the more effective because it would be unsuspected in the convincing reality of those all tough men.

A surprising number of Torrey stories trickled out through 1946 and even into 1947. Nearly two dozen, with a final appearance bylined John Ryan in the May, 1947 *Super-Detective.* After that, the silence of the grave fell over his literary career. A rumor somehow got started that Torrey had been shot and killed by a jealous husband, who found the writer in the arms of his wife. But the truth was more prosaic, if equally tragic.

Eventually, Roger Torrey was virtually forgotten—until pulp collectors rediscovered his old half-remembered stuff. Gradually, some of his work was brought back into print and Torrey's reputation, virtually nonexistent for decades, was re-examined and reevaluated.

The Complete Cases of Johnny Cass reprints all five Cass stories, with the character's original name restored where necessary. Also included is a non-series entry, "Curtains for Five," first printed in the July 1, 1934 issue, in the middle of the regrettably short run of Roger Torrey stories in *Dime Detective*. All six of Roger Torrey's *Dime Detective* early contributions appeared in 1934, indicating his status as regular contributor. While Torrey returned to the magazine for four additional tales in 1939–40, Johnny Cass/ Carr did not reappear.

For reasons that may never be known, all of his 1934 *Dime Detective* stories carried the clipped byline, R.D. Torrey. He never signed his work that way again.

The stories in this collection showed Roger Torrey in his prime. He was fond of the series character, but he rarely let one run more than a handful of years, then he would abandon them forever and create a new protagonist. He often had more than one hero running concurrently in *Black Mask* and other titles.

Like Dashiell Hammett, who had also rubbed shoulders with the criminal element, Roger Torrey depicted an authentic if disturbing world. This world still survives to this day, but it is radically changed. Torrey's stories show how it was nearly hundred years ago.

His fellow honky-tonk musician turned pulpster, James Moynahan, once put the writer's work into proper pulp perspective when he asked:

> Is the pulp writer's best work lost on the average pulp reader? You can't very well expect people of mature taste to wade through pages of Screaming Skulls, Crimson Corpses, or even teak-jawed private shambuses *[sic]* with lean napes, who hard-heel through page after bloody page, clipping, rapping, and grating at inoffensive set-ups who have the ill-luck to get in the path of the famous detective. Any more than you can expect school-children, elevator boys, and the people who "read them just for relaxation" to get the most out of Mr. Torrey's stuff. His verisimilitude is lost on many, but Mr. Torrey is the sort of writer who wins out.

This very collection proves Moynahan's words to be true. Here is Roger Torrey at the top of his game—taut, tart, tough, and as solid as a hard-boiled egg. Or yegg.

OPALS ARE UNLUCKY

DETECTIVE CASS LIKED MR. SANDBORG THE MINUTE HE MET HIM BECAUSE HE HAD SUCH A SWELL SMILE. HOW COULD HE TELL THAT TOOTHY GRIN WAS JUST AS PHONY AS THE REST OF THE SET-UP? THAT THOSE GLEAMING MOLARS WERE GOING TO BRING HIM AS MUCH GRIEF AS THE OPALS THEIR OWNER WANTED?

THE DESK buzzes me and tells me a Mr. Sandborg is coming up and I tell them to let him come.
I know it must be business because any friend would have
sailed past the desk without going to all the fuss and there's
no sense in asking them what he wants because I can find
out when he gets upstairs. I go over to the desk I got in
one corner of the room and pretend to be busy and when
I hear the rap on the door I call: "Come in!"

He does. He's a big smooth-looking monkey with the
color hair that's between white and yellow. Straw I guess
it's called. His eyebrows are white. He's got a mouth like a
trap but the minute he smiles I know I'm going to like him.

He says: "You're John Cass?" and keeps smiling. He's
got big white teeth and this smile shows them all besides
crinkling up the corners of his eyes and making dimples
in his cheeks. I don't like dimples one bit but I smile back
in spite of myself. He hauls out a card case and passes one
over and says: "I'm Herman Sandborg. Portland, Oregon."

The card says the same thing.

I TELL him he's right about me being John Cass and tell
him to sit down and he does and I look him over trying to
figure him out. He's money even in Chinese. He's dressed
like I wish I could with everything matching perfect, the

whole thing crowned by a gray hat that looks like the hat ads. Like a hat never does for me after I wear it once.

He sits down and takes a cigar case out of his pocket and offers me one, bites the end off another as he stares around the apartment. He lights it and says: "I rather expected you to have a big office from what I've heard of you, Mr. Cass."

I ask him: "What did you hear and from who?" and he says, never stopping smiling: "I've heard you take cases that you don't talk about afterward. I heard this from Myers at the Olympic Insurance and Indemnity Company. I do quite a lot of business with them and asked them for information. Does that introduce me?"

It does but that grand big smile of his would have anyway, so I ask him: "And you have a case for me?"

He says: "I think I have. At least I want to hire you."

I sit back and let him go ahead.

He rolls his cigar around his mouth while he stares at me and then he says: "You know Farmer Sheats?" He's watching me close. I've known Farmer for five years or more, just the same as I know every hustler in town. I don't mean the small change but the number-one men. I just nod.

"How well?"

"Pretty well. I spend a few dimes in his places once in a while when I'm flush."

I can see he knows Farmer is about the biggest operator in town and I figure it's a beef over losing some dough. This Farmer runs wide open and gets a big play on just about every gambling game there is or ever was. He's got 'em all.

"Friend of yours?"

"Well, I know him."

"Take a case that'd mean bucking him?"

I start slamming but he just grunts.

I lean over and tap the desk in front of him and I say: "Mr. Sandborg! I'll take a case against anybody if"—I make the 'if' big—"there's a legitimate case against him. Get that legit? Licenses are too hard to get and too easy to lose for me to fool around. As far as bucking anybody, I work for money. Does that answer you?"

I guess it does. He stares at me hard and says: "It's your town, Mr. Cass. I'm just feeling my way."

I tell him: "O.K.! Sheats ain't too tough, if that's what you mean."

He nods again and stares up at the ceiling and tells me: "He's got something I want or I've got something he wants. I came down here after some correspondence between us to try and do a little business. I've talked to him and I'm..." He hunts around for a word, starts to say "scared," but says "worried," instead. I don't say anything and in a minute he goes on with: "It's harlequin opals."

I ask: "What are they?"

He looks back from the ceiling at me and grins. He says: "Darn few people know what they are. That's a fact. It's a peculiarly marked opal, in brief." Then he goes on for about ten minutes giving me a lot of dope about harlequin opals. I finally stop the lecture by saying: "I see."

HE LOOKS back at the ceiling. I find out this is a habit of his when he's trying to figure what to say and how to say it. He comes out with: "I've got an almost exact mate to a stone this Farmer Sheats has. Either one by itself is valuable but paired they would be worth much more."

"Same as pearls."

"Exactly. Now I want to buy his and he wants to buy mine."

I say: "Can't you get together?"

"We talked a little bit at his place of business on Spring Street and I went back to my hotel after making an appointment to see him at his house tonight. I was followed back."

He jerks his eyes back from the ceiling quick to see how I take this and I nod at him and ask: "But where do I come in?"

"I want protection in case of any attempt at robbery."

Now I like this big boy and I don't want to rob him myself. Besides that, running around with him as a nurse couldn't run into more than twenty a day and I'd be charging just double rates if I charged that. Unless there's a chance for dough I don't like to play so I tell him what to do. I say: "Why don't you leave it at the hotel and change your date to some time tomorrow and make it at some jewelry store. You'd be safe that way. I don't want to take your money on a false alarm like this."

I figure it's a false alarm. I can't see Farmer going that route.

He nods very thoughtful and says: "I'd thought of that but I must go back to Portland. I'm a retired lumberman but I still have interests that demand my attention. And besides—" He hems and haws a bit and comes out with: "You see, Mr. Cass, a collector doesn't always inquire too closely into—well—you know. We're all the same." He kind of blushes and wiggles those white eyebrows and his smile looks sort of ashamed. He waves his hands and goes on with: "I really wouldn't care to go to a jewelry store and chance—"

I laugh, can't help it. He thinks the stone he's got is hot and is too bashful to say so. I say: "I'm sorry but I don't see a chance to make a dime off you. I wouldn't want to go out to Farmer's house with you on a fake like this. Farmer'd think I'd blown my cork."

We talk probably another half hour and I buy a couple of drinks and make him see that Farmer Sheats is too big an operator to go for the rough stuff. He finishes his drink and finally puts on this dandy new hat of his and I goes to the door and shakes hands with him, tell him what a pleasure it is and the rest of the hooey and promise that if I ever go to Portland I'll stop out and see him and he goes and I go back and take another drink. At that, I ain't lying when I say it's a pleasure. I never saw a man I liked better so quick.

It's about seven thirty then.

I go down and get a bite to eat at Sampsel's place right off Alvorado and by the time I get back to the apartment it's about eight thirty. I sit around for a while figuring whether I'll go to a show or go out on Redondo and see some friends and by the time I make up my mind it's too late to do either so I decide I'll go to bed and read a while.

I'm in pajamas and have got the wall bed wrestled down and here's another knock.

I go to the door and see it's Sandborg again and I tell him to come in. I see his grand new hat is dirty and that his hair is mussed when he takes it off. He comes in and tosses the hat on my bed and says: "It happened. Just like I knew it would. Just as I started up the walk to the house."

He's damn near crying and I ask: "You get the business?"

He sits down on the bed on top of his hat and puts his head in his hands and nods and says: "It's gone."

I say: "Tough!"

"If you'd only gone with me."

I say: "If the dog hadn't stopped he'd have caught the rabbit."

"Listen, Cass!" He takes his head from between his hand and stares at me. "If I wanted wise cracks I'd go to a show. I want action."

I'M WALKING on my heels from the bang I get out of Farmer pulling a stunt like this but this starts to smell like money to me and I come to quick. I say: "What kind?" and stare back just as hard.

"I want that stone back. I don't care how you get it. That kind of action."

"What's that crack mean?

I can see he's got a little bruise over one cheekbone. Not big, maybe the size of a quarter.

"I heard that you"—he figures out a nice way to put it!—"you go on a case and get results and that you use odd methods at times to get them."

I say: "You mean..." and he waves his hand at me to stop me and says: "I don't want to know anything about how you recover it."

"I see. You want this rock back for how much?"

Whoever he talked to about me could have told him that when it comes to money talk I spit out what I mean. He says: "Five hundred. It's worth that to me."

I laugh at him.

He says: "Seven hundred and fifty," like every word hurts him.

I tell him: "A thousand and expenses. You to pay expenses whether it's dice or no dice but no grand if no stone. How's that?"

He thinks a minute and I go to the kitchen and pour him a drink. He looks like he needs one. He takes a nice big swig and kind of shudders over it and then he says: "All right. It's a deal."

He keeps on sitting on his hat and on the bed like he wants to talk about it but I start to the door and say: "Where can I get hold of you?" I've got things to do and I don't want to talk about it.

He takes the hint and gets up and puts on what's left of his hat and tells me: "The Biltmore."

I say: "O.K.! I'll call you. This happened out at Farmer's house, is that right?"

"Just as I was turning in. I'd sent the cab away."

I tell him O.K. again and he sails out and I get dressed. I think when he's going out the door that that hat of his will never look the same. I also think that it's a gut the stone would still be in Farmer's house because he'd never take a chance on packing it around with him.

I know better than to try and put the finger on Farmer myself. I'd be behind the eight ball if he smarted up and he's a smartie. The Lord knows why he's called Farmer because he ain't one. I go down to Moe Bernstein's pool room and look around and here's the guy I'm looking for playing on the third table in.

I give Arlie the eye and he comes over. I say: "Hang up the cue, big shot. There's work to be done."

He must be ahead of the game because he grins. He hangs up the cue and covers the most ungodly striped silk shirt I ever hope to see with a coat that'd run a close second to the shirt. He's three steps ahead of the styles at all times and he's outdone himself on this outfit. This Arlie, he calls himself Arlington Andrews, I suppose because his name is Arlie Epstein, is a smart little boy from St. Louis. He's back there and gets a screwy notion that he'll come to Hollywood and drive all the sheiks out of pictures but he's handicapped by having a schnozzle that Durante wouldn't be ashamed of and a pimply face that looks just like one of these actors he's so rabid about except for not having no chin or no forehead. He looks all right except for this. He's plenty smart though and does just as I tell him so I use him for tail stuff once in a while when I got to have somebody. He's getting by on what little I give him and his pool playing so you *know* he's smart.

I take him outside and to the car and ask him does he know Farmer Sheats. He says he does so I give him ten bucks and tell him to hang around Farmer's Spring Street place because that's the biggest and that if Farmer ain't there when he gets there he'll be in before they fold up. I tell him to phone my apartment the minute he sees him and that if he don't get me the first time to keep on calling. I know that by the time Farmer closes up and counts the take I'll have time to go out to his house and have plenty of time out there before Farmer can make it home.

I PUT the kid in a hack and send him on his way and drive down to Eleventh Street and pick up an old-time yegg I know named Dummy Zein. This Zein is an old-time cracksman that I got out of a jam once and I know he'll do anything I want him to do… as long as I'm along with him for protection. He's lost his guts.

He's home as I know he'll be. He's called Dummy for a damn good reason. He says: "What you want?"

I say: "You."

He says: "What for?"

I say: "A job.?

He says: "O.K."

That's all there is to it. He's got his tools in a trick vest that looks like a carpenter's apron only it's built higher up and he grabs this and we go. He sits in the car just like a clam and when we go up to the apartment to wait for Arlie to phone and I offer him a snifter he don't even grunt. He just reaches out his hand. It worries me about that kit of his and I say: "It might take soup."

He don't say anything to that either, just reaches in his vest pocket and pulls out a medicine bottle with some yellow stuff in it. He waves this at me and I waves it back and plenty quick. He acts like it was water.

I hate to wait around like this but Farmer's got a habit of sticking at home in the evenings and just going down to check up and I can't take a chance. He's dingy about his wife. I know that if I make a mistake with Farmer I'll be behind the eight ball right then and there so I don't fool. We sit around, Zein with this glum look on the dead pan he sports and me fidgeting around plenty. I'm afraid to take any more to drink because if there's going to be action I can't afford to be slowed up.

About twelve thirty the phone rings and Arlie says: "He just come in and started to check up on one of the wheels that folded up about eleven when the play quit. What now?"

I tell him to go on back and shoot some more pool and Dummy Zein and I start for Farmer's. I know Farmer's got two more wheels, three blackjack and as many more poker games and Lord knows what all else to check up on and know that we got at least two and maybe three hours out there. I also know Farmer and his wife live by themselves and that she's smart enough not to make a fuss if she sees we got the edge. I figure to get the edge. I been out there once with Farmer and I know the set-up.

We slide out Beverly until we come to Ardmore and we turn down there a couple of blocks and I leave my Ford coupé under some trees and Zein and I get out and walk down to the third house from where I leave the car. I been scared to death all the way that some drunken fool might crash us, and us with that soup that'd blow us sky high.

I don't fool around in front of the house because nothing looks so phony as some monkey stalling and looking around so we turn right up the driveway toward the back door. It's all dark and Dummy follows me like a pet poodle. He ain't said why or where or one damn thing yet. We get to the back door and some pooch in the house next door barks a couple of times but outside of that there ain't a sound. I ease up on the back porch and try the back door and find it's locked. I look at the lock and see it's a spring lock that can't be got into with a pass key and step to one side and point it out to Dummy. He makes the first noise then he's made since we leave the apartment. He grunts.

He takes out a spring-steel arrangement from under his coat and slides it alongside the lock and leans on it. It's pretty thin. Then he takes one that's damn near as thin as paper and diddles around for a minute and we're in.

I put a handkerchief over my mouth, nose and chin and tie it and give another to Dummy and leave him in the kitchen. Then I take my flashlight and pussyfoot into the bedroom and there's the missus dead to the world. She's a good-looking head, maybe thirty-five or thirty-eight. I take a piece of tape from my pocket and lick it plenty and slap it over her mouth which I thank the Lord is closed and she wakes up and stares at me in the light of the flash. I say: "O.K., lady, you ain't going to be hurt if you don't make no fuss."

I makes my voice deep and try to make it sound like I mean what I say.

She's got all the guts in the world. She just nods and looks at me.

I say: "It's no snatch so don't get fussed."

There's been a regular epidemic of snatching hustlers or their wives and I don't want her to think she's in too tough a spot else she might get desperate.

She nods again.

I whistle soft for Dummy and he comes in and I point over to the corner and he goes to work.

FARMER'S GOT a nice little can—to keep the baby's pennies in. It's not tough because everybody knows he don't bring any dough home with him and I guess he figures he don't need a good one. It's not one of those round affairs that are tough but a little square business that might just as well be made out of tin as far as Dummy's concerned. Farmer keeps the thing in his bedroom which I figure is another mistake. In case anybody does want to crack it they might crack Farmer on the head along with it with him being close like that.

I've heard all about the way the deed is done but this is the first time I ever see it. Dummy takes a little breast drill that comes in sections out of that trick vest of his and puts it together. Then he bores away for half an hour, all around the lock with me sitting in a chair and watching him and the gal at the same time. He gets through with this and goes over to the bed and takes off the blanket that's draped over the foot of it. He takes some putty and builds up around the lock with this and pours a little of the stuff that's in the bottle into this. The surprise to me is how little he pours. He fools around some more with the putty and then fuses it and hangs the blanket over the whole thing.

He strikes a match and the gal looks scared and I don't feel so good.

I say: "We'd better scram?"

Dummy looks as much disgusted as the upper part of his face will let him and says: "Oh nerts!"

He touches her off and comes over by my chair and the gal pulls the covers over her head and slides as far to the other side of the bed as she can. We wait about a minute and the can goes: "Tunk!"

I swear you couldn't have heard it in the next room. All that happens is that the blanket jumps a little bit.

Dummy goes over and yanks the blanket off and the upper part of his face looks pleased. He grunts again and I can see the lock sticking out of the door like a pop eye. He goes to work fooling around and in a minute he's got the whole lock out and laying on the floor and in another minute he's got the door open.

It takes just forty-two minutes from the time we come in the house. I timed him. Of course the box was easy, not even having an inside door, but still and all it's a pleasure to see an artist in any line of work.

Dummy starts to put his stuff away and I look inside the safe. I know just what I'm looking for and in a few minutes I find it. There's a lot more stuff there but I don't touch none of it. There's even about five hundred in fives and tens there that Farmer must have for getaway money if he needs it and it sticks to my fingers like glue but I leave it. I stick the opal in the little case it's in, in my pocket and wave Dummy out to the kitchen and say to the gal: "You got any alcohol in the place?"

She nods.

I say: "Ether would do it easier but that'll do. Wait about ten minutes after we're gone and take that tape off with it. No hard feelings, sister."

She nods again and stares up at me. If I ever find another gal with the cold nerve that Farmer's wife has got and she hasn't got a face that'll stop a clock I'll get married myself. I swear that if that tape hadn't been on her puss she'd have grinned at me.

I slide out to the kitchen and collect Dummy and we blow out to the car. We make it O.K. and I take him back and drop him and tell him I'll pay him off in a day or two and get the last grunt of the evening. I'll say one thing for Dummy, he don't crack wise.

I call Sandborg at the Biltmore and tell him to drag up to the apartment right then and he seems perfectly willing. It don't take him over twenty minutes. I can see from his eyes that he hasn't been to sleep yet though his clothes look like he's been lying down in them. He says: "What now?"

I say: "You got twelve hundred and ten dollars on you?"

He asks me have I got it and I tell him I have and he says: "I'll have to go back to the hotel."

I tell him O.K. and that when he comes back with the dough I'll have the stone for him and that the two ten extra was expenses. I figure I don't want to be seen with him in case Farmer's wife has called Farmer and he's put a tag on Sandborg. I tell him to do a little switching just in case and how to go to the Arcade Building between Sixth and Seventh and walk through there in a hurry and take the first cab he sees and have it drop him back at the Biltmore and walk through one entrance and come out the other and get another hack there. This Farmer is just tough enough and can pull enough weight that I don't want him in my hair.

He says he gets the idea and that the expense money is O.K. and smiles at me with that big grin of his and for a minute I think it don't make any difference even if Farmer does smart up. It's like being hypnotized.

He comes back with the dough and pays off just like a slot machine. We damn near kiss each other saying good-by and he goes back to his hotel and I go to bed.

EVERYTHING GOES fine and dandy the next three days. I stick the grand in my deposit box and pay Dummy the two hundred and go on with my business. I haven't got a thing on the fire and I'm following the papers close to see what I can chisel a case out of.

I'm out on a false alarm trying to get a little action on a divorce case over in Pasadena where an old man gets framed by his young wife that's nerts about some other guy but the old boy won't go for it. The funny part is that I know how he was framed and the whole thing and can prove it with little work but I'll be damned if I do it for nothing. I gets back to the apartment about nine that night and I'm just burning up at the old fool that I talked to and at myself for being fool enough to talk to him. I slam into the apartment and reach for the lights and just as I snap the switch somebody jams a gun in my guts and says: "Steady!"

I stand steady.

I look over across the room and here's Farmer and his old lady and Arlie and Arlie looks just about as sick as I figure I must look. There's a smart-looking monkey standing close to Arlie and Arlie's got as pretty a shiner as I ever see in my life. It hangs clear down to his mouth and wiggles some when he tries to smile at me. I peek around and take an eye at the boy scout that's got me foul and he's just as hard as the guy that's by Arlie. Maybe harder.

We all just stand there and by and by Farmer says: "Is it him, Mary?"

Mary takes a good look and says she isn't sure.

Farmer says that maybe she can tell by my voice and tells me to say something and I say: "Now listen, Farmer! What's the beef?"

She says: "He talked deeper than that."

I take a good long look at Arlie and he hangs his head and I say: "What the hell, Farmer! Why put on an act? I'm it."

There's no sense in me stalling. I could see they'd got to Arlie and I might have known they would. I'd told the little fool to keep his mouth shut but he didn't know the score and in that minute I figure how he probably brags around to some of his cheap hustling friends about how he spotted Farmer Sheats for his friend, Johnny Cass, the private dick, and that Farmer puts his ear out and picks this up. He gets hold of Arlie and gives him the works. One look at Arlie's pan tells me this.

Farmer says: "If you'd been rough with my wife, Johnny, you'd go out now. She says you treated her easy. That plain?"

I nod. I feel sick and plenty sick. This Farmer's got enough connections to make it plenty tough for me even if he don't give me the whole works and he ain't above that.

I figure I'm behind the eight ball right. He says to these hoods of his: "Shake him down and take the punk out in the kitchen."

They do it and take a gun from under each arm. Then they hustle poor little Arlie out in the kitchenette.

Farmer says: "Sit down, Johnny, and let's talk this over. I don't get this deal at all. We always got along if we didn't kiss each other in railroad stations."

From his voice I can see he don't get it.

I sit down and look at him and his wife and wait for him to go on. I know better than to make a break with those two hoods just the other side of the door.

He says: "What in hell is the idea in cracking *me* for that opal. You working for Sandborg?"

There's no sense in lying about it so I nod yes at him.

"I could lose you your license for this, Johnny, if I want to talk to the right people. If I make a charge you'll go up."

Now I'm in no shape to talk back but this bums me plenty. I say: "*You* should make a charge. How'd *you* get it?"

He looks at me puzzled. Then he says: "I bought it from Engelman's on an order. Two years and more ago. What's that got to do with it?"

I SEE the whole thing then and am I really sick. I thought I felt bad before but that was nothing. I can feel my face getting red. I say: "Then you didn't get it from Sandborg?"

Farmer says: "Hell no! He's got a mate to it but he wanted twelve grand for it and nine's a fair price. Ten at the most. We couldn't do any business."

He must figure right then what I've already thought out. He says: "So that's the angle. He told you I robbed him of it, is that it?"

I nods.

He looks sort of sad and says: "I thought you knew me well enough to know I don't go those routes, Johnny."

I tell him: "He asked me for protection first and the way the play come up I fell for it. It seemed O.K. at the time. I didn't know."

Farmer thinks hard for a minute before he speaks. "That was worth nine grand, Johnny, like I told you. You got that much?"

I tells him no.

"Can you get it?"

I tells him no again.

"Then what about it?"

My mind has been working faster than it ever did before in my whole life though anybody with what you might call a mind wouldn't be in such a spot. I say: "If I get it back what then?"

Farmer thinks hard again. He's got a long smooth horse face that doesn't show what he's thinking. If it's thumbs down I'd never know it from him. He finally says: "In my racket I know better than to hold a grudge. I can see this is a mistake. It'd be O.K."

"Will you give me a week? And let me go out of town?"

He thinks again and I see his eyes sort of shine when he turns to his wife. He says as if he's surprised at himself: "I'll be damned if I don't, Johnny."

I can see he's thinking about something funny. He grins at her and then at me and says: "Don't say a word. I know just what you're going to do. But Johnny will you do me a favor?"

I say what and sure.

"Knock those pretty white teeth a yard down his throat."

I say: "Yes, but not for you." I can see he remembers Sandborg.

He calls his hoods in from the kitchen and they give me my guns back after we compare the address that Sandborg leaves with me with one on the letters he's been writing to Farmer. They jibe. They go out then and leave Arlie with me and I look at Arlie and he looks at me.

Finally he says: "I couldn't help it. They had me between them and they'd have killed me."

He was half bawling. I was going to ride hell out of him for letting off his flannel mouth about spotting Farmer but I didn't have the heart and just tells him: "O.K. Arlie! We're going to make a trip. Anything you want to take?"

He says: "I got a lot of clothes where I room."

I say: "You can take one suitcase and for God's sake don't take that trick suit. We're not joining a circus."

He looks hurt and helps me pack a bag and we're ready. I get a hack and drop him at this place where he lives and tell him to meet me at the station and then I beat it down to Eleventh and tell Dummy to get set for a trip.

He says: "Now?"

I say: "Yes."

He grunts and starts loading up. He holds up this trick vest of his and looks at me I nod and it goes in the suitcase and we're out of there in five minutes and down to the station in another ten with fifteen to spare before train time. I get a section and another lower and Arlie comes along. Right there it starts.

He says: "Didja see in the paper where that big tramp of a whoziz gets a new contract and a grand a week to go with it? And is he a tramp? Why say, if I couldn't do better than that…? and on and on and on until the gate opens.

By this time already I'm sick of it. It gets worse on the train so I go to bed two hours earlier than I want to.

WE LAND in Portland about three in the afternoon and check in at the Benson. I figure somebody's going to pay the nut on this trip and anyway if you go to the best it looks better in case of a beef. And I figure it can well be that.

The first thing I do is look up where Sandborg lives in a car I hire from a Drive Yourself and then I sic Arlie on this heel of a Sandborg. Then Dummy and I sit around for three full days with me figuring whether I'm going to blow my cork or not with him just sitting there and not saying a word. It's either a feast or a famine. The only time he ever talks is when we go and eat and then he says: "Same." That's all. I swear it.

I can't even let go and take more than a few drinks because I never know when Arlie will give the high ball.

Arlie says this lug goes from his house to his office and from his office to his house and that's all so I make the break instead of waiting any longer for it. We go down to the Drive Yourself place, that is Dummy and I do, and pick out a little sedan that's got an ordinary paint job that nobody'd notice and we start out. Sandborg's office is right by the Orpheum Building and there's a garage in the same block where he leaves his car so I figure I'll pick him in between. It's on Broadway and a plenty busy street but I figure that if I work it right there won't be a rumble. We park between about four thirty and I put Dummy in the driver's seat and one gun in my pocket and we wait. By and by I see him coming.

Now this Dummy Zein is funny. He'll crack a box and that's all. He won't do one damn thing else so I have to. Sandborg's about ten feet from the car when I step out and join him and ram my gun into his side. I push hard too. I say: "In the car!"

For a minute it looks like he's going to make it a party. He stands there and I can hear his nice white teeth grinding and I say low to him: "Maybe Myers at the insurance company told you I'd use a gun," and ram harder. I don't know what I'd do if he backed up—I don't think I'd have shot but I don't know because the minute I see him I just burn up. It's a hot spot for a minute, people trotting by and two cops on the other side of the street and another not over fifty feet away and coming towards me.

Whether it's because Myers at the insurance company *did* tell him or whether he's smart enough to figure how hot I am I don't know but he grits his teeth and gets in our car like a little man. He's so mad his face is white and he's sweating like a pig. I can see drops of it hang in those white eyebrows of his and sort of shiver there. Dummy is watching us with that dead pan of his and when we climb in the back he gets us out of there.

He's with me when I case Sandborg's house and knows the way. It takes fifteen minutes and I'm telling Sandborg what the score is every second of the time. He ought to learn it by heart.

We stop in front of the house and the two of us get out and leave Dummy in the front seat and he leaves the motor running. This heel lives in a swell place and when we go in the hall I see a gal in a maid's uniform at the far end of it but Sandborg don't crack and I keep my head down so she can't see my face. Sandborg don't pop because I've got about three inches of a .45 barrel in his short ribs.

He turns into a room that's on the right and I see it's a library with a nice big honey of a safe. One of the new ones that'd even stump Dummy for a good long while. Sandborg squats in front of this and goes to work but he's so damn mad his hands are shaking and it takes him about ten minutes to open it. I don't ride him about this because I can see it's no stall. He gets it open and drags out a leather case and I can see there's two of these trick opals in it and he picks out one and hands it to me but it drops and rolls under the table. I make him crawl under the table on his hands and knees and he sets the case with the other one on top of the safe. He gets the opal and comes out with it and hands it to me and I reach out my left hand for it. That's where I make my mistake. He's been watching his chance.

He grabs my left wrist and jerks me to him and catches my gun with his other hand. He starts to bend the gun down but he's got hold of it in such a way that he can't quite make it and in such a way that I can't shoot. We just stand there face to face and working plenty hard. He sees he can't win that way so he lets go of my left hand and grabs onto the gun with both of his and starts bending it down. That leaves my left hand free and I start slamming it into his belly just as hard as I can but he just grunts and swings in close so I can't hurt him. He's got thirty pounds on me and he's just like nails.

I swear I hurt my hand on his belly muscles.

I FEEL the gun sliding down and the trigger guard starts to raise hell with my trigger finger that's caught in it so I try a new one. I sag and start to give him the gun figuring that when he eases I can pull away but it don't work. He don't ease. He just holds me up and takes the gun away from me.

He gets it and starts to lift it and I kick him in the hand that's holding it and plenty hard. The gun sails over to the other side of the room with him right after it as if he's afraid I'm going to try and beat him to it.

Not me. I just haul the other one out and wait until he gets over to it. I'm never so thankful in my life that I carry two. He gets there and I say: "Leave it lay!"

I'm afraid to talk out very loud because of getting everybody in the house in there and I'll never know whether he didn't hear me and understand or whether he heard me and decided to take a chance. I don't care. He's got his back to me when he picks it up and he's got it raised and swinging on me when he faces around.

I can't see it's any time to fool around and try any trick shoulder shots or hooey like that. His face is about the size of a dinner plate and about twenty-five feet away and I bore him as near the center of it as I can hit. He comes down on what's left of it like somebody drops a sack of wheat. All in a bunch. I drop the opal he gives me right after the brawl starts and don't figure I've got time to look for it so I grab the case that's got the other one in it and stop by him and turn him over to get my gun. He's fallen on it and I can't leave it because the number is registered on my concealed-weapon permit.

And then I get a shock.

I turn him over and find I've caught him right in the puss. I shoot a .45 and it's made a hell of a mess and on the floor underneath his mouth in a lot of blood are these pretty teeth he showed so damn much of when he smiled. Uppers and lowers. Both false and both smashed. I pick up the gun and the teeth and take a powder.

I look down the hall when I come out but there hasn't been time for anybody to get there yet so I make the ten feet to the door in a hurry but when I'm outside I walk slow and easy to the car. Dummy has heard the blast and has got the door open beside him and we pass two guys and a girl about fifty feet down the street but they don't pay any attention to us. All they're doing is listening to the screams that start to come from the house. I watch back and see that they don't try and catch our license number so we're all O.K. They may get in the excitement but it'll be too late to drag us in. We leave the car at the Drive Yourself place and ease back to the Benson and wait and along about nine there's an extra out that clears up plenty.

I hear 'em shouting it from the window so I send Arlie down and he comes back with it.

It says that Sandborg was killed all right but it also says as how his safe is open and that the police in looking around looked through it and find out that Sandborg was a high-class fence and that most of the stuff in there is stolen and that he's got a record as a con man on top of that that'll stretch from Portland to Los Angeles. The best thing is that the law figures he was killed by some hood in a row over stolen property.

And me thinking he was such a swell head.

We get the morning train out and when I get to my apartment I leave word for Farmer at all three of his places and his house to come up and he comes up in about three hours. All alone. He comes in, looks at me hard for a minute and says: "I see you clicked."

I say I did and pass him the opal and ask him if that's it. He kind of frowns and looks it over with one of these eyeglasses jewelers decorate themselves with and admits it's right. Then he says: "I read in the paper about it."

I say: "I did too. Must have happened after I left."

He grins and shrugs his shoulders and I pop for a drink. We chew the fat a while and finally I get expansive and give him half my souvenir. I give him the uppers. He gets up and starts for the door but the gift must have touched his heart because he stops and says: "If—mind you, Johnny, I say if—I should get that other stone at auction I'll see that you get your expenses. But only if I do." He stares at me hard and ends up with: "But I wouldn't figure on the dough too strong. I can only bid it in if it's auctioned, or, if it was stolen buy it off whoever it was stolen from, if I get a break."

I tell him that's fine but I don't figure on it. I should worry. I don't do bad. After paying Dummy and Arlie for all the time they're away from the city and expenses and all I still got about seven hundred of Sandborg's dough and that's not bad money for making a mistake.

I always hear that opals are unlucky and I guess they are—for Sandborg.

HOT MONEY

WHEN THAT EX-CON WALKED
INTO HIS OFFICE AND SPILLED
THE DIRT, DETECTIVE CASS
THOUGHT IT WAS JUST A LITTLE
BUSINESS OF HOT MONEY THAT
COULD BE COOLED OFF IN A DAY
OR SO. BUT HOT MONEY CAN TURN
INTO HOT LEAD AT A MOMENT'S
NOTICE HE SOON FOUND—AND
WAS NOT TO BE COOLED EXCEPT
IN A BLOOD BATH MADE FOR THE
PURPOSE.

HE AIN'T more than halfway through the door before I pick him as just out. Not so much from the waxy look his skin has got because lots of people have got that but just from the way he looks at me. He looks like he's trying to see something coming at him in time to duck it. He stands just inside and says before he closes the door: "My name's Collins, Mr. Cass. Tom Collins."

I tell him to close the door and when he does I ask: "Folsom or San Quentin or are you supposed not to know what I mean?"

He grins very weak and says: "McAlester, Oklahoma, Mr. Cass. And McNeils Island too."

McNeils Island is Federal and they don't board 'em there for breaking into baby's bank. It's mostly for bad money and up. Collins holds the shaky grin and asks me: "You remember Sam Koslinder?"

I do and I tell him so. Sam made a bunch of twenty-dollar bills that were very *very* good. Almost good enough to get by. He even almost had the right paper.

He says then: "I knew him at the Island. He said you were okey and that I could speak right out."

I tell him that when I see Sam I'll buy him a drink for the build-up. I'm safe enough because Sam is doing life under the habitual-criminal law. He used to be a good Joe before he went off the track. I wave at a chair and tell Collins to sit down and spit out what he wants and he sits down and starts it. And what a yarn.

IT SEEMS that this Collins, whose name is really George but who has always been called Tom, after the drink, goes with two boy friends and breaks into one of Uncle Sam's post offices and makes a mistake and leaves fingerprints around Uncle's safe. This is in a little town here in California called Tracy and some years ago. Ten, to be exact. His boy friends leave some prints along with his, maybe so Tom wouldn't feel bashful. They get eighty dollars and about that much more in stamps for this master crime and drift back east to Oklahoma. They get back to a little town called Hobart and get ambitious and daylight some little bank there which was a mistake because the bank's got an alarm connected with the local law office and when the boys get outside they meet the law coming over. Tom makes it to the car with the loot but his two boy friends get picked up. There's a traffic jam in the excitement, same as there always is, and Tom gets clear away. Then the local law checks up on his pals and finds that Uncle wants them here in California and tell 'em that they won't rap 'em on the bank job if they'll turn Tom and the loot up. The boys go for this, very naturally, and Tom gets nailed but not until he gets clear back to California and stashes the loot. Then Uncle tries the three of them on the post-office job and they all get ten years. All three get out after they do seven of them but Oklahoma law's waiting for Collins with extradition all fixed up and Tom goes back and does another three on the bank job. He'd have done more except the judge took the seven just served into consideration. His story that he don't remember what he's done with the bank money don't get over so good but I guess back there, after the James boys and the Dawson brothers and a few more of those old-timers, they don't take a bank job to heart. Anyway, he does another three back there and the loot is still loose.

He tells me this in a kind of dull voice and never looks up from the floor until he's got it finished. All the time he's twisting his hat like he's trying to wring water out of it. Then he says: "I want you to get the dough. I can't."

I reach over and take what's left of the

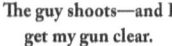
The guy shoots—and I get my gun clear.

hat away from him, though it's too late to do it much good, and ask him why not, and he tells me that his two friends are camping on his tail for one thing and that either some law from Oklahoma or some insurance-company dick is trailing all three of them. He figures he won't split with his pals because he thinks they shouldn't have turned him in for one thing and that he figures they wouldn't split with him for the other. He thinks they'd take it all. And the law trailing all of them complicates this because he *knows* the law would. It seems that one of his boy friends has turned out into a first-class hood, one of the hired-hand class, and he admits, though he don't have to, that he's lost his guts.

When he starts talking about this friend of his, his voice gets shaky and he starts to sweat so I believe him when he says he's scared of him.

I tell him that it's no dice. That getting stolen money back for the guy that stole it is too far off-side for me. I explain that I'd lose my license on that kind of play at the very least and that probably I'd make ail-jay along with it. I make it sound as nice as I can because after all he's a friend of Sam Koslinder's and Sam and I used to be chummy before he finds out what a swell racket making money is— or ain't. I don't get the angle about Sam sending this guy to me because Sam knows damn well I don't play these kind of games but it ain't the guy's fault and so I smooth it for him even if I am half sore.

Collins looks at me very patient and says: "Oh it's not that, Mr. Cass. I want you to return it. And get the reward."

NOW HIS story gets better than ever. He says he knows he shouldn't have the dough and that he wants me to take it back and that he would himself except that he's afraid to get it and afraid they wouldn't pay him the reward after he *did* get it. He's right on this last. He says that after putting

in ten years between the two prisons he figures he's enti-
tled to keep a little of the dough. The insurance company
that covers the bank has paid off long ago and he's got the
notion that sticking the insurance company for part of the
reward for returning money he stole himself is perfectly
O.K.

I explain to him that I run a pretty straight business
and this stuff ain't and even if I should put in with him
and play this on the straight side I'd be likely to have too
damn hard a time explaining *how* straight I'm playing it.
Jail birds is jail bait as far as I'm concerned and this stolen
money smells.

As far as sticking the insurance company being all right
goes he agrees with about ninety per cent of the people I
know—most people seem to think they should get a medal
for hanging something on one of them. I don't because if
for no other reason I do a lot of work for them. As far as his
yarn, I know there's a standing reward out for the recovery
of stolen money so that checks. If it wasn't so shady I'd go
for it but I just can't do it.

One thing sticks me so I ask: "Why pick me for the
act? Sam must've told you I wasn't playing these kind of
games. Don't you know anybody that'd help you on it and
split the dough with you? The reward will only be twenty
percent and I don't get your angle in going for it. Why not
the whole thing."

He says: "There was twenty-eight grand. If you go get
it and give me half the reward it'll make twenty-eight
hundred or close to it. The money is the full-size bills that
was used before this small money come in. I couldn't pass
it."

I'd forgot all about that. He'd play hell trying to put
twenty-eight grand or any part of it back in circulation

with his record. He's half smart at that, figuring twenty-eight hundred is better than nothing.

He meauws around some more and tells me to think it over before saying yes or no and I tell him it'll *still* be no dice but to come back tomorrow night and maybe I'll have some angle figured out where he can keep in the clear. I feel sorry for him but I just don't want in. I tell him tomorrow because I want time to check on the yarn a bit and see if there's anything he's forgot to put in. I know enough people in the record offices, both at the Central Station and the sheriff's office to be able to do this. He says he'll be back some time after nine, just depending on how long it takes him to shake off his tails, and gets out.

I check the yarn and finds out it's just about as he tells it. His record was clean before the post-office steal and so was the two boys' that was with him on the job. They switch though. In the three years since these two are last out one of them is taken up three times but don't get anything hung on him. His name is Gus Partin and he's pretty hot, according to the guy I talk to. This guy Gus is one of the lads that hang around North Main, that is, the North Main spots, and he'll do anything he's big enough to. I look at his picture, he's been mugged, and figure I'll know him if I see him. I've got to do all this without putting out any information so I don't find out as much as I want to, but I figure to keep shut and let this poor devil of a Collins get a break for himself as long as *somebody'd* get the reward.

This night I sit and wait from nine to eleven but I don't worry any because I figure Collins is probably making sure he's lost his tags. Right at eleven I'm in the kitchenette mixing a short one and this slows me up on what happens in the hall. I've got a ginger-ale bottle tipped over the glass when I hear the first shot. By the time I get the bottle and glass down on the drain-board I hear the next one. By the time I get to the kitchen door I hear the third. Spaced even like that—the way somebody shoots when they're calling their shots. While I'm grabbing a gun of my own I hear footsteps pound past the door and by the time I get the door open and get out in the hall I can hear 'em past the bend. I see somebody laying on the hall floor and know it's Collins, by a hunch, and chase after the footsteps and miss by one floor because I see the indicator on the service elevator swinging from three to two and I'm on the fourth. I know the elevator opens within ten feet of a door that opens on an alley and know it's a cinch there's a car there waiting for the shooter so I beat it back to Collins who's as dead as a man can be. He's got two holes in his chest and when he drops from these the guy boomed him through the head. There's about fifty people out from their rooms and milling around the hall and the manager and a clerk and all this inside of a minute of the shooting. Pretty soon there's a lot of law and after I find out that Collins hadn't asked for me at the desk either that time or the night before and that the clerk don't know he was looking for me I fold up and go to bed, figuring that the thing is no dice.

I can't fool around on it myself because he didn't tell me where the dough was hid the night before. It's just too bad as far as I can see and while I think I'll give McAndrews of the homicide squad a tip the next day about looking up Collins' boy friends I can't see why I should mix in it. I don't work for the city of Los Angeles but for Johnny Cass and who hires him.

This is on Tuesday night.

ON THURSDAY I get a letter signed Mrs. Collins and saying that she knows about Tom coming up to see me and will I go and see her. The address is between Second and

Third on Carondolet, not such a hot neighborhood, but the letter seems okey and I figure to take a chance though I may be running into something. Whoever shoots Collins must know he was on his way to see me and they may figure I know what the score is, but the letter don't say to come at any certain time and I figure I'll make the play during the day and that even if it's a plant I ought to come out all right.

I make the turn from Second onto Carondolet and about halfway up the block I see two police cars and an ambulance and maybe half a dozen other cars parked close enough to see the fun. There's a bunch with short-wave sets in their cars that do nothing but cruise around and follow the prowl cars in this town. I pull in front of the ambulance and when I do out comes a couple of internes with a gal on a stretcher and after them McAndrews. He spots me and comes over and I say: "Mrs. Collins?"

He says: "Uh-huh! You looking for her?"

I say: "Right! How bad is she hurt? How come a homicide man is out on this?"

He shrugs his shoulders and looks mean and says: "I got a hunch it's tied in with her old man getting killed in front of your apartment. She ain't hurt bad. That is, she hurts plenty but she ain't hurt, if you know what I mean."

I say: "Where they taking her?" and he says the Georgia Street Hospital will get her. Then he opens the door of my coupé without any invitation and says: "I want to talk to you, Johnny, and I want to get the right answers. I was going down to see you and this saves me a trip."

I TURN the coupé and head back to my apartment. On the way there he tells me that one of the heels that was working on Mrs. Collins had took the muzzle of a gun and kept rapping on her nose until he had it spread all over her face but that she'd pulled loose from them and got a chance to sing out for help. I tell him that I'll remember that and use it myself sometime and he says: "If you get a chance to use it on the same guy that worked it on her remember to break his wrist along with it. He did hers."

I say: "Who was the guy?" and he looks sourer than ever and says: "Hell—that's what I wanted to talk to you about. She won't say, except there was two. She says she don't know."

We go up to the apartment and I pop for a drink and he says: "What was Collins up here for? Don't say he wasn't here because I got a guy that saw him come out of here the night before and he wasn't ten feet from your door when he got the business. I been checking up."

I say: "Another drink, Mac?"

He says: "Like that! You're going to keep secrets too, hunh."

Mac's a pretty good friend but he's an honest cop and I figure that if I crack about what the angle is he's liable to give this Mrs. Collins a little hell. He'll figure that maybe she's in on where the money is and will go to the mat with her to find out *just* where. It ain't my put-in and I don't take any chances. I tell him that I don't know what the score is but that I figure I'll see Mrs. Collins and find out and that if I do and it's anything that'll do him any good I'll turn loose with it. After all, he's on homicide and looking for the shooters instead of why the shooting. He don't believe the stall and after telling me he don't he rides down with me to the receiving hospital. I go in with him, I can't lose him, and introduce myself to her and she don't say anything in front of him except that she wanted to ask me if I have any idea who knocks over her old man. She's pretty smart at that. She looks at him and gets the angle about keeping quiet and in spite of being half high on the dope they give her to cut the pain she don't crack.

I can see I'm going to like her and I can see just as plain that Mac ain't. We sit there a few minutes and I tell her that when they turn her loose for her to come up to the apartment and she says she will and Mac and I get out. We're standing by my car and he reaches over and taps me on the shoulder and says: "I went and checked up on the gal, too. She wasn't in on any of her old man's work and she makes a living in a restaurant jumping counter. Now give me a break, Johnny. If you know who's after her like this, tell me and let me put 'em away. That's working for her and for me too. Be nice."

I can't see it'll do any harm to give him a tip.

"Pick up Gus Partin then and see if he knows where he's been and what he's been doing the last few days. This is just a guess but he might be mixed. Is that a help?"

SOME PEOPLE might put out a thank you for a tip like that but Mac is good for a go to hell instead. He snaps out: "You ——! You're going to clam up at the wrong time some time and I'm going to kick the devil out of you in a back room down at the station. Is that the guy that worked on Mrs. Collins?"

I say: "Mac, it's just a hunch. It might be. Tell me before you do the kicking so I'll know."

While I'm getting in the car I see him beating it back into the hospital to a phone and I know that before I get back to the apartment the finger will be out for Gus Partin. Mac is old-fashioned as hell when it comes to beating up women.

The next day up she comes. She's a little woman, not over a hundred pounds, and she's wearing a heavy veil and a pad over her nose and one arm in a sling. She's maybe thirty-five but looks older. She comes into the room looking back over her shoulder like she's afraid of somebody sneaking up behind her and this gets my goat plenty. I took it to heart what Mac said about her making her own way and it burns me up to think she's got to be afraid to even walk through an apartment hall. I sit her down and tell her that her husband didn't tell me he had a wife and she tells me that he probably didn't figure it made any difference. Then she just sits there looking at me until finally I have to open.

"What did you want to see me about, Mrs. Collins?"

She's got one of these thin voices that sound like she's afraid of running out of breath. She hurries toward the end of each sentence.

"Tom said he talked to you about helping him and you wouldn't. Please won't you do it for me?"

Doing it for Tom and doing it for her are two separate things. I don't know what else he told her and I don't want her to make any mistakes. I say: "If I do, we'll return the money after we get it. You understand that?"

She says in that quick hurried way: "Oh yes. It isn't *my* money."

I nod my head and tell her that Tom spilled out the whole story and she says:

"If you'll go with me now we'll get it."

I say: "Now?"

She says: "As well now as ever." Then she looks around at the door to see if anybody's there to get her. She's scared sick but trying to hide it.

I say: "Sure! Excuse me while I dress up more."

I wear a shoulder harness that carries two guns sometimes. Most shoulder holsters, if they're the spring kind, let the muzzle of the gun slide away from you, toward the back of your coat, when you pull down on the gun butt and I got a vest fixed with a little buckle that fits to the bottoms of the holsters and stops this. Some of the rigs have got a hickey that's supposed to go around your belt but they're never long enough to reach it. If you're standing straight it's no help but if you're stooping or falling or anything like that it might save a hang. The rig does take a minute to get into, though, and she acts like she's in a hurry. To get her mind off this I speak to her from the dressing room.

"You ain't said yet who it was got rough with you."

I can see her in the mirror in the door that's half open and I see her shake her head. She purses up her lips kind of before she answers.

"I'm not going to. This is bad money and it's caused too much trouble already. It's a temptation and I'm going to remove it."

This helps place her. I think she's one of these religious cranks that'd choke on a bite of dishonest bread—if she wasn't pretty damn hungry.

"Why didn't you tell McAndrews, the big copper that was talking to you with me, and let him help you? He could get this as well as me," I say, just to keep her busy.

I can see her face tighten up and I change my slant some. She comes back with: "And have the insurance company get nothing. It wasn't and ain't Tom's money and I'm going to see that it's returned to them that *does* own it."

I don't laugh but I've got a hard time not to. I say: "You don't trust the law too much, do you?"

And then while I'm getting on my coat over the guns she tells me how she knows for a fact that the copper on the beat in front of the hash house she works in takes graft from a speakie and a Chinese lottery joint that are in the same block as the restaurant. She admits that she don't think he gets to keep all the dough but has to give most of it to the guy over him in charge of the district but that don't smooth it down too much for her.

I say: "You know if you were tagged up here?"

When she looks blank I say: "I mean followed."

She gets kind of proud then and sniffs: "Tom spoke of that and I was very careful. I rode on a street car clear over to Boyle Heights and looked in store windows for a while. I don't think anybody that was following me would be apt to think that I was coming right back over here."

She might be right on it at that. And it gives me yet another slant on her too. She's suspicious and she's tight-mouthed and she's a damn fool on top of these. I figure she's got nerve, though, and that's something. Then comes the kick. We go down and get in my car and when I ask her where to go she says: "On Pico between Alvorado and the next street. We—uh... Tom..."

I say: "Go on."

She says, and gets plenty red, so red I can see it through the veil: "When Tom and I were living together, before he was arrested, he—uh..."

I say: "What?"

She says: "Bootlegged."

I say: "Oh my God!"

SHE GOES on for all the time it takes to go to Pico about how at the time she hadn't realized that the money they made was bad money and all the rest of the same kind of screwy argument and all the time I'm half listening to her and trying to see if we're being followed by anybody. There's a yellow cab that seems to be hanging close for a while and there's a Buick coupé that also acts phony but it's hard to tell and so I think I'm just fussy. I finally shut her up on the sermon about bad money by telling her no money is bad but that some money is hot. She thinks this over while I click down Pico for a ways and keeps her trap shut and by and by points out a house that's set a little ways back from the street and still looks like a bootlegger's house.

I say: "You know who lives there?"

She says she don't.

I ask her how we're going to get in then if she don't know 'em and she looks at me disgusted and says: "You're a policeman, ain't you, or you can say you are."

Another slant and not such a bad one.

I go up to the door after looking up and down the street and not seeing any car that looks like it was tagging us and when I knock a guy comes to the door that looks plenty fly. This is a break because I ain't got any business knocking on strange people's doors intending to go in and take out twenty-eight grand even if I *am* intending to return it to the people it belongs to. I look at him hard and say: "What's your name?"

He says: "Well, I... George Wessel."

I say: "Where you from?"

He says: "Uh... uh... San Francisco."

I say: "Don't give me that. Move back."

He starts to say something about this and then he changes his mind and steps back and I make motions at Mrs. Collins to follow me and we're in. The front room is shabby as hell, has got two davenports and a big table that's marked with white rings around where the table cloth don't quite cover it, and there's a bunch of kitchen chairs at the table. I know that the house hasn't changed—it's still a spot. This Wessel starts to say something and I say just in time to stall a beef: "How long you been running? I don't mean the joint, I mean you."

He says: "Hunh!"

I say: "All right, all right, your hard luck! I'm trying to be nice but it ain't no use. I'll show you it don't pay to put up no argument with the law, guy."

He gets white in the face and kind of stammers out: "I ain't getting tough. Honest"

I JUST get my bluff in first is all. I'm taking chances on plenty of trouble when I tell him I'm law but I can maybe stall this off by explaining to the judge that I mean private law. Maybe. I figure better have no beef. I take him over in the corner and get real confidential. I tell him that I ain't really after him and that I may give him a break if he's nice. I explain how I'm looking for something big—I make it sound big too—and that such small potatoes as a pretty good guy selling a little inky-drink don't worry me if I'm not annoyed by anything. A swell line and it goes.

He waves his hand at us and gives us the place and Mrs. Collins and I leave him in the front room and go into a damn dirty bedroom and she closes the door and shows me the door casing at the side and how to jerk it up a couple of inches and then it just lifts over and out. She's still got the sling on her broken wrist. This lets into the space between the wall of the front room and the bedroom and I can see it ain't been used for a long time. She tells me it used to be their liquor plant. There's no light in there and I strike a match and there on the floor, covered with dust and dirt, is the dough. Just laying there loose. I haul it out and we put it on the bed and count it out into a pillow slip we take off the bed and I suppose seeing so damn much money all in one piece like that slows up what I think with because when I hear the front door open it don't register the way it should.

I got my side to the bedroom door, though, and when *that* opens I pay attention plenty. There's a guy standing there, trying to get the layout like a man does when he goes into a new place, and when I see the gun in his hand I go sideways so's at least to give him a moving target and yank for the gun under my left arm with my right. This takes me within a couple of feet of Mrs. Collins and on her right side which is the one she's got the good arm on. She's standing by a little bed-table. Just as the guy in the door shoots—and misses—and I get my gun clear—something bangs me on the right shoulder. It's hard enough to numb the arm and I drop the gun. I about half go on my ear and kind of turn toward her as I catch myself and I see her coming down at me again with the table lamp she smacked me with the first time.

I MANAGE to get my right arm up far enough to take the most of it again on the shoulder but I get a pretty solid smack in the ear just the same. I get the gun under my right arm just as this mugg in the door shoots and misses again, but when I look at him to try for one on my own side I know I'm going to get the lamp because I can't dodge the lamp at the side and shoot in front at the same time. I manage to get in one while it's coming down, though, and I go down but not out. Just dazed enough not to be able to move. I get a hazy impression of Mrs. C. bending over the man in the doorway and I know I ain't missed like *he* did because he's on the floor and it's a bullet instead of a lamp that's put him there. Then in another flash I see this yegg of a Gus Partin, I can tell him from what I remember of his pictures, coming in through the doorway and reaching down over the guy on the floor and pulling Mrs. Collins up and taking a smack at her. I try to snap out of it enough to raise my gun but I can't make it. Gus catches her right between the eyes and she comes straight back and lands on the bed like she'd been thrown at it. She lands about half on the sack and he shoves her over and looks in the sack and goes out the door with the sack we made out of the pillow, just stopping along enough to kick me in the ribs. He steps on the guy in the door as he goes out which'll show how careless he is with his feet.

I hear the front door slam and the bootlegger comes and stands in the door with his mouth open and I manage to tell him to bring a glass of water. I'm up by the time he's back with this and I toss it in Mrs. Collins' face and she comes to and goes over to the guy on the floor. And I'm watching her plenty close to see she don't boom me again. I don't have any idea why I got it but it don't seem like a good time to ask questions.

When I shot at the guy I aimed center but I must have been trying to dodge the lamp when I let go because I've only got him high in the right shoulder. The .45 I shoot hits hard and the shock has knocked him colder than a wedge but he ain't really hurt and he starts to come to with her bellyaching about how hard he's hit.

She's sitting on the floor with his head in her lap and the bootlegger is trying to pad the hole in the heel's shoulder with a towel that'll give him blood poisoning sure as hell and a lot more people come in. I know it ain't no use for me to start out after the guy when he took the powder with the money because I'm still dizzy as hell and if I caught up with him it'd just be too bad so I'm just sitting on the bed thinking things over and wondering whether I ought to take the towel away from the bootlegger. So when the two cops dash in there I am and still with no story. There's a little short, important looking guy along with the two coppers in uniform and he comes over and says: "Who're you?"

I look at him and ask him what in hell does he care.

This makes him mad. He sticks out his chest and says: "You'll find out soon enough."

"I'm a deputy sheriff. You're under arrest."

One of the coppers looks around at him then and tells him to slow up, that if any pinches are made he'll do the pinching. This copper is some guy I've seen but can't place, a big red-faced husky-looking boy. The little guy fumbles around his hip pocket then and finally comes out with one of these cheap nickel-plated Spanish revolvers that sell for seven eighty-five on sales, the kind with a fake ivory butt, and points it at me and at the same time pulls back the corner of his vest and shows the cop a buzzer. He says—

"I'm arresting this man. He shot this man."

He waves the gun past me and at the guy on the floor and then he says to me: "Put up your hands."

He's got the gun cocked by this time and he's taken up damn near all the tension on the trigger while he's waving it and I get my hands up so damn fast I think my fingers'll fly off. Anybody that's dopey enough to buy one of them guns is screwy enough to shoot a man with it.

The cop says kind of soothing: "O.K. O.K. Just let me see that badge, will you, chief."

He walks over to the guy's side and when he gets close jams down on his gun hand and shoves it over and takes the gun away from him. And then he tells him plenty. He explains that he's in charge and that he's got the situation well in hand and offers to make him eat the gun if he makes any more fuss and goes on and tells him that he knows who I am and that I'm a pretty good Joe and that I ain't doing anything at the time that I shouldn't do, like waving a gun around free and easy. Also he says that anybody that's fool enough to deputize anybody like this little guy should ought to have to go around with him and watch him. Then he looks back and tells his partner to give the ambulance a ring and when he sees that Mrs. C. is still holding the guy that's shot but is damn near ready to pass out herself and so is safe he comes over to me and says: "And now, what's your yarn, Cass?"

I ASK him how he knows me and he tells me he's seen me around with McAndrews and I suggest he call and get Mac down there and save some time. I tell him that Gus Partin is the guy that just took the powder and that Mac wants him and how the whole thing's happened up to now because with the shooting and all the rest that's happened unless I come out with all I know I'm going to get jammed. He calls Mac and comes back and looks at the little guy disgusted and then turns to me.

"This little so and so was right outside during all the time this happened and saw Partin get away and never makes a move to stop him. Deputy sheriff. Phooey on such sheriffs."

The little guy says then that he wasn't sure what had happened and that after following Partin and me down he just stuck around to see could he get a break. He says that Partin slid out the door and into the Buick coupé that I thought I saw following me so fast that he couldn't have stopped him if he wanted to. He says then that he ain't afraid of any man in the world and I believe him. He ain't smart enough to be afraid! By the time that Mac gets there, which takes him about ten minutes, the ambulance is there but all we let the interne do is put a patch on the heel's shoulder and when Mac comes in I take him to one side and tell him the lay. I've got the copper to leave the guy there because you can't talk and talk right in a hospital with nurses and all around. I've tried to talk to Mrs. C. and get the reason for the smacking and all that but I ain't got any answers that mean anything and I got a notion the guy that's shot will know 'em. We send her out with the two coppers and Mac and I take the heel with the bum shoulder and set him on the bed and start in.

The guy looks kind of a weak sister and is shaky as hell with the shock the slug gave him and I don't figure we'll have any trouble and we don't. Mrs. C. is his sister, that's the reason she smacked me so I wouldn't shoot him. He was with Partin when Gus worked her over up on Carondolet but he's so scared of Partin that he's afraid to try and stop him and that also makes sense. Then we ask him where Gus lives and he says that he and Gus have got a room in some two-bit lodging house by Ninth and Maple. Mac looks at me and I look at Mac and Mac calls out front for the two coppers in uniform to take the guy up and hold him on an open charge until we get back and we go outside and head for my coupé. When we get opposite the prowl car that the coppers have along Mac stops and says: "Wait! The guy'll have to go to the hospital and he can ride up in the ambulance first class with his sister to hold his hand. We can take one of these boys with us."

I figure it's a good stunt, this Partin's bad, and why take chances? We pick the guy that give me a break inside and just then I miss the little guy with the trick gun. I says: "What happened to bozo?"

The copper says he beat it off in his yellow taxi that was waiting. He looks sorry and says that he didn't know he ought to have held him and I tell him that it's okey and that we'll find him pretty damn soon. We tell him where to go,

Ninth and Maple, and Mac and I get in back and all the way Mac rides hell out of me for not stopping Gus when I have the chance and gets a hell of a bang out of me being too sick to do the pursuit act. He believes it, though. I've got a banged up ear to start out this one with.

INSTEAD OF a lobby like a regular hotel you climb up to the second floor and pass by a table with a register on it and a bell above it with a sign on it telling you to ring for service. Gus has got Room Eighteen according to Mrs. Collins' brother and we go down the hall toward it, the three of us, Mac and I in front and this red-faced uniformed boy bringing up the rear. We go plenty quiet and when we get there and hear talking inside we stop and listen. The walls of the dive are no thicker than pasteboard and every word comes out plain.

Gus says: "You smart little…. Ever see so much dough in your life?"

We hear a thump like something being tossed down on the floor.

The smart little… says: "You can't do this."

Gus says: "Maybe I can't but I am. How you like this?"

There's a harder bump and a kind of meauw out of the little guy and I figure what I figured was going to happen is happening. I had the little guy picked as a fool from the first word he speaks and I knew damn well that if he come up by himself and braced Gus what'd happen. I don't give a damn about the little heel and I hold up my hand to Mac to listen some more and right then the copper behind us sneezes. Nice and loud. There's no more noise from inside and me being closest to it I hit the door as hard as I can with my shoulder, figuring it's locked, and it's open and I go too far in and stumble and fall over a suitcase Gus has been packing on the floor. I get a picture of the little guy sitting on the floor by the head of the bed and holding his nose and another of Gus at the side and pawing for a gun in a shoulder harness and right then Mac follows me in and is on Gus.

I see Mac smack him in the face with his gun and Gus comes down to the floor with us two already there. I'm sitting in a bunch of money that's been knocked out of the suitcase and I start picking it up and putting it back in and Mac sees Gus is knocked colder than a wedge and puts the copper to watching him and comes over and helps me. Then the little guy starts crying about his trick gun that Gus has taken away from him, as I know he would, and the copper searches Gus and finds it in his pocket and gives it back to the little heel, who's now yapping about having a busted nose.

THE SUITCASE is one of these little black affairs, just about big enough to hold the money is all, and about the time we get the dough back in and the bag closed Mac has to go to the door and tell the landlady he's the law and it's a pinch. He tells her to call the wagon for him and while he's busy chewing the fat with her I see that Gus is coming to and I go over there just in case he comes out of it tough and puts up a battle with the copper, and by the time Mac comes back from the door and we talk to Gus a minute I look around and see that the little guy ain't in the room any more and neither is the bag. His second sneak.

We make it out in the hall about the same time, Mac and I, leaving the copper in uniform to watch Gus, and I see that the law is being called by the landlady like Mac has told her to. She's standing at the top of the stairs holding the phone and there ain't nobody else in the hall at all. In these bum hotels they keep to their rooms if there's trouble. When we get to the top of the stairs we see the little guy just making it out to the street. Mac calls him to stop but I'm not wasting any breath on anything but getting down the steps. I get to the street about ten feet in front of Mac and here's the little guy about fifty feet ahead and just getting ready to cross it. And then he proves he's a fool. He reaches for this back pocket of his again and fumbles out that trick gun and I shout at him to stop but he takes a crack at me. I stop running when I see the gun, about thirty feet from him, and Mac's about even with me when the little heel turns loose. Mac sits down on the sidewalk. I wouldn't have believed a man in the world could hit another man at that distance with a gun like that but here it is. Then he proves it's an accident after all. He shoots twice at me while I'm leveling and then I take him in the ankle, aiming for it on purpose.

He's dropped the bag in the gutter when he hauled out his gun and he kind of totters and falls on top of it. He shouts out for me not to shoot him any more and I look down at Mac and see him holding his leg above the knee with both hands and talking at the top of his voice and I know he won't kick in right off at least, and so I go over to the little heel and kick his pea shooter out in the middle of the street and grab on to the bag. I see the traffic cop from Seventh and Maple coming up the road on a run and I wait for him and tell him to watch the little guy so he can't run off any more and then I go back to Mac and send some kid down to the hotel where Partin and the copper is still parked to tell the copper to have the wagon pick up Mac and the little guy on the same trip. Then we all wait for the wagon and as soon as it comes and is loaded I grab a cab and go to the Hellman Bank.

I go from here to the telegraph office and wire the bank back in Oklahoma to see what insurance company they was covered with and while I wait for an answer I go up to the jail and have a heart-to-heart talk with Mrs. Collins. I know they're holding her up there and will until Mac gives her an okey, she being picked up with her brother and all.

Here's where I get her angle on the money and the whole thing. She tells me that she knows all the time about her brother being mixed up in the thing with Gus, but that he's the kid brother she's always looked out for and she kind of blames herself for him being mixed up. It seems he met Gus through her dead husband. She thinks that if she gets the dough out of harm's way and out of any place that Gus and the kid might get hold of it that Gus'll leave the kid alone.

This all checks with the idea I've got of her being a good pal with the wrong people. I tell her that if she'll make out a complaint against Gus on a torture charge, along with the one that Mac'll swear out with it, Gus won't bother anybody for a long time and then she starts fretting about what's going to happen to brother. I tell her that brother'll also be out of trouble, probably for three years, and that it'll be a good thing for her and brother too. She cries plenty about this and I tell her I'll go down and talk to Mac and see if I can get him to make it easy on the kid.

MAC IS laying there about half asleep from the shot he gets when they dress his leg but he snaps out of it and talks to me and tells me he hasn't got a broken leg but only a bullet through the meat. He says that the little guy has a broken ankle that'll keep him in bed for two months at the least.

We talk over the whole thing then and there and try to decide what in hell is the matter with the little monkey.

Mac says that the little guy *is* really a deputy sheriff from the Oklahoma town where the bank was knocked over and is deputized here as a courtesy. Then we try and figure what the little devil was trying to do with the dough. He claims that he wants to return it to the bank and collect the reward but Mac and I both decide he went screwy when he saw so much dough and decided to take a chance on collecting it for himself. He ain't smart enough to see where he'd get caught in trying to pass that much in those over-size bills. He's about half out of marbles, we figure.

Mac says that as far as he's concerned, the way it's all come out, he's willing not to say anything about the little guy blowing his cork and this is okey with me. Then I tell him about Mrs. Collins and get a bit of an argument.

I tell him that I'm going to split with her just the same as the original deal her old man wanted to make and he says that she hasn't got any part of it coming to her and that as far as he can make it stick, brother's going to get all that he can hand him. I make a talk right back and tell him what he told me in the first place. About how she's working hard and is just a damn fool trying to save a weak brother that she's nuts about for no sane reason and finally this line about gets over. After all, she didn't have anything to do with stealing it and it would still be out if she hadn't helped as she did. Mac says he can fix that part but what about him.

I say I'll split my cut with him and he says no but that if I want to put five hundred out he can use it. He's married and too honest to really knock down and I don't blame him for figuring he's got a cut coming. If it hadn't been for him I might have got over and I might not have. I probably wouldn't have got to Gus Partin's hotel in time to stop the get-away he was getting set for. It ain't like graft, it's a present for taking a slug that was meant for me. I figure this is legitimate but when he says: "And are you going to pay the little guy from Oklahoma's hospital bill too?" I burn up. I say: "Don't be a fool!"

He says: "You shot him."

I say: "And I would again. If a heel takes out with hot money and gets shot while he's making his sneak let him find some more hot money to pay his bill."

Mac grins and says: "Maybe you're right. It might not *pay* his bill."

I figure that money, hot or not, will pay a guy's hospital bill when he's shot, but not my hot money. Mine goes back to who it belongs to. That is, except my cut.

A DEATH IN THE FAMILY

IT LOOKED LIKE SUICIDE—AND
SHOULD HAVE BEEN—THE DEAD
WOMAN'S HUSBAND BEING WHAT
HE WAS. BUT THERE WERE ANGLES
THAT POINTED IN ANOTHER
DIRECTION, DETECTIVE CASS
FOUND, ON TAKING A SECOND
LOOK. ANGLES WHOSE CORNERS
WOULDN'T SQUARE UNLESS THE
SUM OF THE SIDES EQUALED
MURDER.

THIS MAKES the sixth night that I sit there and try to eat and try not to listen to them dig at each other. Just little mean remarks that don't mean a hell of a lot by themselves but show what the score is. He's got a big, boomy voice and she's got a little, whiny voice and every time they speak they get in my hair so that I figure this is the last night for me. If I can't eat in peace I figure it's time to quit.

It starts out like one of the ordinary run of the mill things. He telephones me and I go and see him and he tells me that he's scared and wants somebody for a nurse. I ask him what he's scared about and he stalls and tells me to sit tight and work at it for a week and if I haven't figured it by that time he'll tell me. I figure it's a false alarm but I also figure he's good for the twenty a day and expenses that I ask for, and besides there's nothing else doing. Twenty a day is twice what I should get, but he never says a word. So I start living with him, going to the office where he's supposed to be running a wholesale linen factory in the morning, going home with him at night and eating with him and then going out chippying with him. I bet my expenses, if I paid them instead of him, would have run into plenty on this last. He knows every clip joint in town and gives 'em all a play, and after the first time I tell him he's being took and he tells me he knows it, I don't say a word.

After twenty minutes at dinner the first night and I hear his wife I know where he's getting the dough and I figure out who he's scared of about the same time. She makes a crack about how a man that cheats on his wife is better off dead and follows this up with what the Bible says about the same thing. She's nuts about him and she's got the bankroll and she's nuts about religion… the eye for an eye kind. Also she's got a sour pan that don't match and is about ten years older than him so I don't know as I blame him much for chiseling.

This night she says:

"Shall we have our coffee in the other room?" the same as she always does, and he says: "Sorry, dear. I have to check on that last shipment," the same as *he* always does. That is, he always stalls though he changes the stall each night.

She sniffs and says: "Blonde or Brunette, Henry?" and he gets red in the face and says to me: "Shall we go, Mr. Cass?"

It's "Mr. Cass" when he's with her but it's "Johnny" when we're alone or brawling. I don't think he's told her I'm a dick that's supposed to be guarding him because she curls up her lips at me and says: "I'm disappointed in you, Mr. Cass. I had hoped you would influence Henry toward a *better* life, rather than drag him down."

Just a nice girl taking her Sunday cut. Any man that could drag Henry down would be a honey and she knows it. It's my turn to get red and I say: "Now, Mrs. Martin! I hope—"

She don't even give me a chance to finish it. She whines: "I suppose your girl is red-headed."

We get out.

WE MAKE the usual rounds and he gets half tight and I take about two more than I should and we take the gals home and this gives me an awful bang. He's called up some friend of his and told her to get a girl for me and she turns out to be a red-head. All the time I'm with her I keep thinking about what Mrs. Martin had said. We start home about two with me doing the driving, because he never takes the chauffeur with him when he's catting, and on the way I tell him that I'm going to quit. This

Martin comes up and says: "My God, she's killed herself!"

sobers him up plenty. He says: "But I'm afraid. You know what I'm afraid of."

I say: "You're nerts. She's too crazy about you to kill you."

He gets very solemn then. He says: "Did you ever see her mad?"

I say: "No, thank God."

He says: "She's just like a crazy woman but I'm not afraid of her when I'm with her because I can talk her out of it. I keep thinking that she'll hire it done."

I don't say anything and he goes on and tells me that he thinks that lots of guys would kill a man for a couple of thousand dollars.

This is funny. I know a lot that'd kill a man for a hell of a lot less and think nothing of it. If I didn't think she was so nuts about him I might believe him. I say: "You're screwy. Why would she?"

He says: "If she gets one of these mad spells and thinks about religion at the same time it'll just be too bad. She'll sacrifice me"—I see him make a face in the light that comes from the dash—"on the altar of her love."

I tell him he's eppus but he ain't so screwy at that when I think about it. I've got her pegged as being just about ready to blow her cork but I never think of this angle. I don't blame her so much at that, for she must know he's married her for what dough she has and must figure that as long as she puts it out she's living up to her end of the bargain and that when he steps out he isn't. I think about this for a minute and decide that I should worry about either of them. I don't particularly go for him even when he's buying me drinks and I don't go for her at all. I think about the frozen-faced butler and how I hate his guts, and about the pleasant line of chatter that's handed me and I say: "I quit. Tomorrow."

He says: "Why? I'm paying you what you asked."

I say: "I left home when I was twelve because my old lady and old man battled all the time. It makes me nervous. Besides, I don't like the late hours."

He sighs and sits back in the seat and we pull in the driveway.

They've got a big house that's set back from the road in a bunch of trees and there's a drive that winds up in front of the front door and then goes back to the street so you don't have to back the car. He gets out and opens the front door and tells me to leave the car there and let the chauffeur get it in the morning and when we go into the hall he says: "Well, we'll talk about this in the morning," and I tell him sure but I'll still quit.

All the bedrooms are on the second floor and as you go down the hall, his is the second on the right and mine the third. His wife has got the first, the one with windows fronting on the street. I watch him go in his door and I go in mine and take off my coat and the harness I use to carry two guns. I'm just sitting on the bed when I hear a funny noise outside. It sounds like a bump and if I hadn't been about half stiff I'd have probably looked right then. I don't though, and have got one shoe off and am leaning over the other when I hear him call: "Mr. Cass!" in the next room.

I dash in there, hippity-hop, one shoe off and the other on, and see him leaning against the dresser and the window open. He points out the window when I come in and I stick my head out and see a guy running toward the front of the lot. He's about ten feet from a clump of trees but I shoot once, just for luck. And I know I miss the minute I let go. I keep craned out the window for a minute, hoping he'd cross the driveway and give me a break but he don't and I can't see any sense in chasing him so I turn around to Martin and say: "What happened?"

He's holding the top of his head with both hands and he says: "He was hidden in the closet and when I opened the door he hit me with something. It didn't knock me out but dazed me so I couldn't move. When I was able to say anything I called you."

His voice *had* sounded funny but that might have been from coming through the wall. I say: "Where'd he hit you?" and he shows me his head and there's a place there that he says is a bump. I know that a sap doesn't have to leave a bump when it lands on top of a guy's hair and he couldn't have been hit hard because he didn't go clear out. I say: "Lucky he didn't land on your temple. A sap's bad."

He sits down on the bed and groans and says: "Pour a drink!" and waves at a bottle on a stand, but I say: "I'm going to see how Mrs. Martin is," and walk out and leave him.

I KNOW she's got a wall safe in her room and I think she might have got hurt. I go to her door and knock and she says: "Yes?" and I say: "It's Mr. Cass. There's been a burglar in Mr. Martin's room and I didn't know whether he'd hurt you or not."

She says: "Did you shoot? A shot woke me."

I say: "Yes, ma'am. Did you see anyone?"

I can hear her sniff through the door. She says: "No, and you didn't either. You and Mr. Martin are both so intoxicated you don't know what you saw."

I go back to Martin and find him holding the whiskey bottle like he's in love with it and he says: "Did she?" and I say: "Did she what?"

He waves the bottle and says: "Did she get hurt?" and I tell him: "No!" and go to bed.

I kick myself for not looking out the window when I hear the bump because that was probably the guy going down the side of the house. There's a drain pipe runs right by Martin's window and a good man could go up and down it like a ladder, and if I'd looked I'd have got a clear shot at him. I go to sleep thinking what a hell of a guard I am and wondering whether maybe Martin ain't right and if he is, why the guy didn't kill him and have done with it.

The next morning at breakfast Martin meauws around about what a sore head he's got and she tells him that if he'd lay off the whisky his head would be O.K. and we go down to the office. I been thinking this over plenty. There's something screwy about it but I can't figure what.

We get down there and he says do I still want to quit and I say that I do and he says that if I stay on he'll raise the ante to two hundred a week. I pretend to think about it though I know I'm going to say yes, and he says for me to try it for another week anyway. I say that I will and he says that's fine and calls up the same gal he had the night before and makes another date with her and tells her to get the red-head for me again, which is just dandy with me.

We chew the rag a little bit about the night before and I ask: "What d'ya think was the idea of the guy in your room?"

He says: "She hired him to kill me."

I say: "Then why didn't he, instead of bopping you with a sap? He could have knifed you and you'd never made a sound. For that matter, he could have sapped you hard enough to kill you."

This kinds of holds him. He thinks for a minute and says: "Maybe she just meant it as a warning."

I say: "Why don't you take it?" and he grins at me and starts telling me what a sweetheart this gal he just made the date with is. She is at that. She calls him "daddy" but she should call him granddaddy because he's old enough to be hers. He's made the date for ten o'clock and we're supposed to go out to a road house that's on the way to the beach.

I stick around with him all day and we go home about five that evening and just before we hit the block his house is on a car passes us and I get a flash of a guy I could swear is Tod Debenham. I don't get a good look but I think it's him all right, even if I haven't seen the so-and-so in six months.

We go on the rest of the way to the house and the chauffeur lets us out in front. I go upstairs to wash my face and hands before dinner, leaving him downstairs where he wants to look at his personal mail.

There's supposed to be a butler and a maid besides a cook in the kitchen and I don't see anything of 'em but I don't think anything about it. Sometimes they're at the front of the house and sometimes you don't see 'em until dinner. The place does have a kind of funny feeling though and it worries me. As soon as I change my shirt and collar I go back downstairs to Martin's little cubby-hole that he calls a den but there's nothing wrong. He's sitting there holding a drink and he waves me down to a chair and passes me a glass and I take a couple with him before he goes upstairs.

I go in the room with him while he dresses and he tells me what a brawl he's going to put on that night, all the time talking low so his wife won't hear him in the next room. By this time it's about six-thirty and they eat about seven as a rule. By and by he says: "We'd better go downstairs before we're told to," and grins at me and we go downstairs and into the big room that's off the dining room. He rings the bell for the butler and nobody shows up and after a minute he rings again and just about that time I get smart. I say: "Hold everything!" and head for the kitchen.

There's no smell of cooking in the hall but I hear a little noise and what I see in the kitchen don't surprise me one damn' bit.

The cook's a big fat woman and she's over underneath a table she mixes stuff on, tied up and so damn' red in the face I think she's had a fit. She gurgles at me: "Glug, glug!" sort of, and I see she's got a dish rag stuck in her face and tied there with a piece of string. She can still make a noise but not enough to hear her outside of the kitchen. I take a butcher knife and cut the gag loose and then where her feet and hands are tied and say: "Where's Jonas?"

Jonas is the butler. She tries to talk and can't make the grade and points over to a pantry arrangement at the side.

I HOP in there and here's Jonas on the floor with a welt over his forehead that spells concussion as far as I can see it. I know I can't do anything for him—he's a hospital case for sure—and go back in the kitchen and see the cook's kind of paled down. I say: "Where's Liddy?"

Liddy's the maid. The cook says: "I don't know."

She talks like she has to learn how all over again. I pile back to the front room and tell Martin: "You call on the telephone and say 'I want a policeman.' When you get one you tell him you want a doctor too. Hurry!"

He opens his mouth and looks at me and I say: "Now!" and run for the stairs. I hit the top and go to Mrs. Martin's room. I knock once though I know it's no dice and then I try the door. It's locked and I take a slam at it with my shoulder and then remember the door that goes from his room to hers and go in there and try it.

It's open.

I face a big clothes closet when I look in and Mrs. Martin's looking at me. That is, she's looking at the floor between us. This clothes closet has a lot of hooks and she's hanging on one at the back. Her face is a funny purple and I run over there and feel of her and she's stiff. It ain't bad yet but I've got hold of her hand and the joint at the elbow don't bend any too easy. There's a chair about a foot away from her feet that's lying on it's side and I look at this and say: "Suicide!"

At the same time Martin comes in and says: "My God! She's killed herself!"

Now I think that but I don't see how he knows. I'm in front of the chair. Of course I know how it looks because suicides hang 'emselves and murderers don't usually hang people, but about the same time I take a better look at her face. It's this sickening purple all over but on one side of her jaw I see a place the skin is broken. About this time Martin comes all the way into the room starts to reach up to her and I say: "Get away!"

He stares at me stupid and reaches up again and I take him by the shoulder and spin him over to the other side of the room. I say: "Did you call the law?"

He's leaning against the wall with his mouth open and holding his shoulder. He don't say anything, and I say:

"Did you?"

He says: "Why—why no."

I say: "Well you better. This is murder."

He opens his mouth again and just stands there.

I look again at her and see she's got high heels on and that the back of them or the closet door right back of her ain't scuffed any. Then I know my murder hunch is right. I go over to Martin and say: "We're going to call the law. And we've still got the maid to find." I take him by the shoulder again and shove him out the door into his room. There's a key in the door on her side and I lock the door and stick it in my pocket and he says:

"But you can't leave her there like that!"

I say: "If *I* don't leave her here like that, *we're* going to have a lot to tell the law about why we didn't. We can't help her. She's been dead for over an hour."

This takes hold and he shuts up. I get excited some if anything like this happens, but thank the Lord, I don't get foolish enough to forget that this is murder and that the law's as smart as I am.

Martin's got an extension phone in his room and I call the law and tell 'em we need help. Then I start looking for the maid, which is lucky. The cook didn't know where she was and so I beat it back to her room. She lives on the second floor, same as us, but way in the back, alongside the back staircase. I open the door of her room, after I knock, and don't see her but she's got a bathroom she shares with the cook and I look there. Libby's there all right.

The cook was gagged with a dishrag and didn't do so bad. This Libby is gagged with a big bath sponge that's been squeezed and then filled and then jammed into her mouth and she *ain't* doing so good. She's out cold and when I finally dig the sponge out of her face she don't come to. Any gag is bad enough, but when anybody is gagged so tight they can't swallow good and is left on their back with their mouth filled with water they can't get rid of it. If they try to breathe through their mouth, they can suffocate pretty damn' easy.

I yank this gal out into the middle of the room and work on her just like she's been drowning. After about five minutes of this I hear a siren whining up to the house and figure it's a prowl car that's got the flash. It's too soon for the ambulance but I know these cops all know first aid. Martin's offered to help but he don't know what it's all about and so I don't let him but I need help bad. I say: "Go down and open the door for the law. And keep your trap shut."

HE DOES and brings both of 'em up. You can tell they're both off a radio car by the uniforms. One's a big red-faced Mick and the other's smaller and plenty nasty. I hear Martin running off at the face when they come in and I say to the big Mick: "Give me a hand."

He takes the whole lay-out in with one look and goes to work on the gal without opening his face. Nasty don't. I stand up and stretch—my back's about broke—and Nasty says:

"Where's this body he's talking about? This it?" He looks down at Libby and says: "Why waste time? *She's* dead."

The gal gasps at the same time and makes him out a liar. I don't pay no never minds to him and the gal starts to come out of it stronger and breathes for herself and the Mick says: "Gimme a wet towel."

I wet one in cold water and hand it to him and he takes one end and slaps her on the cheeks with it a couple of times. Her lungs are working O.K. and this brings her to. She opens her eyes and looks up at him and tries to scream. She's pop-eyed as hell yet. He says: "There now, sister. I ain't going to hurt you."

She's just scared because she hasn't got her head to working yet. She takes another peep and says: "Oh... oh... oh... oh!" and wastes all the breath the Mick and I worked so hard to give her. He picks up the towel again and gives her another slap and she comes out of it all the way. She sees his cap with the badge on it and quiets down.

The cook comes waddling in then and the Mick gets off his knees and says:

"She's all right now. This woman can look after her and we'll talk to her when she feels better." He looks at me then and asks: "Who're you?"

Martin busts in then and says: "He's working for me, and—"

The Mick says to him: "Shut up!" and Martin does. The Mick looks at me again and I say: "I'm John Cass, private detective. Working as a guard for Mr. Martin." I point at Martin then and say: "That's Martin."

The other cop says: "*Is* there a dead woman or is *this* the one that's supposed to be dead?" He waves at Libby. Libby's crying all over the front of the cook and she's picked a place where there's plenty of room.

I tell him: "There's another one. Come along."

We go back the hall and I unlock the door to Mrs. Martin's room and we go in. They go right over to the body and start to snoop around and I look around and see all I missed when I was there before.

She's got a wall safe there and the door's open about half-way. The combination is pulled out and is hanging down like an eye that's been gouged and I know there's been a gadget used that fastens on the knob and pulls the works right out. I go over and look at it but don't touch it and when Martin comes alongside of me I keep *him* from touching it. I notice he looks funny. I hear another siren then and the big copper says to the nasty one: "Let 'em in, Dutch! I'll stay here."

I see him look over at us and I know he knows it's murder already and ain't taking chances, but at the same time he ain't going to get tough with nothing to go on unless he's forced. It didn't worry me any because my conscience is clear and I ain't touched anything. Martin's all right too, I think. We've got an alibi up to a little after five and the doctor can tell how long she's been dead and that'll let us out. And then I remember her arm hadn't been so stiff when I felt of her and I don't feel so good.

A surgeon and two internes follow this Dutch back in and in a minute there's four guys follow *them* in and I thank my lucky stars I know a couple of them. They're in plain clothes. I say: " 'Lo, Mac… 'Lo, Tony!" and they both say: "Hi, Johnny!" and come over and shake hands.

Mac is Leon McAndrews and Tony is Anatole Corte and they're both Homicide men. One of the guys with 'em is a photographer and the other is a print man and they both go to work. Mac says: "What's this?" and waves his hand at the body.

I say: "That ain't all of it. There's a guy downstairs with a cracked head and can't the doctor look at him first? I'd have gone to the door and met you but there'd been an argument."

Tony says: "Why would there?"

I say: "This is murder and I don't think the big copper over there would have gone for it. He'd think I might take a powder."

Mac says: "Hunh!" and tells the doc what I tell him about Jonas and where to find him and comes back. He says: "I thought she did the dutch."

I say: "It's murder!"

We all look solemn. Then I introduce them to Martin and they go over to the body while we stay at the side out of the way. The big cop angles back by us just in case we should start to run away I figure, and the nasty one called Dutch just stands and eyes us from over by the door. *He* ain't taking chances either.

The big guy says: "What happened?" and I start to tell him, and then Mac and Tony come back and I start all over again. The doctor calls the two internes and they go down and take Jonas out to the ambulance and then the doctor comes back and starts to look at Mrs. Martin. They've already taken pictures of her hanging there and he cuts her down and looks her over. He gets through and comes over and Mac says: "How long's she been dead?"

The doctor looks at his watch and says: "Killed about five, I'd say. Few minutes one way or the other. *Rigor mortis* is prominent but not complete."

Mac says to me: "And you say you and Mr. Martin got here about that time." He gives Martin a screwy look and I see this Dutch brighten up. He comes over and says to Mac: "Why couldn't they have sapped the butler and tied up the maid and the cook and done this? They was here and you know—" I get the dirty look then,—"how these private dicks are. A bunch of things."

Mac's a very patient man. He heard the whole speech before he cracked. He says then: "You on Homicide or the Radio Squad?" and says it very low.

Dutch says: "Why, Radio Squad."

Mac leans over and taps him on the chest and says: "Stay on it then." You could have heard him for a full block. He taps himself on the chest then and says:

"*I'm* on Homicide. *I'm* in charge here. Get it?"

A detective-lieutenant hates to have a patrolman tell him his business. This Dutch gets red in the face and walks away and his partner snickers. I want to but I'm too smart. I don't want enemies on the force if I can help it even if I never could be friends with a so-and-so like this Dutch.

I SAY to the Doc: "How bad was the butler hurt?" and he tells me: "Partial concussion. He'll be out for hours and probably won't be right for a couple of days." I tell him about the maid and he beats it out to see that she's all right.

Then I tell Mac about Martin getting sapped the night before and he pulls at his lower lip and tells me it's probably burglars. He also says for us to be at the inquest at ten in the morning and not to try and leave before then. Then he takes me over to one side and says: "I'm taking your alibi for Martin now, Johnny. This looks screwy though. That woman was knocked out and then hung, and why would a burglar do that?"

I've been thinking that same thing. If she'd committed suicide I know that while she was strangling her feet would have kicked all the varnish off the door behind her but that panel didn't show a mark in back of her heels and that means she died while she was unconscious. That's plenty plain. I say: "I'll check up on what I can, Mac. Martin couldn't have done it."

Mac says: "Try and find out what you can as a favor then."

I say: "Then we're clear?" and he says: "Sure, but—see you in the morning."

I know if he don't see us then that there'll be murder warrants out for us by noon. I go back to Martin and tell him: "Let's go. We can't do any good here and the cook can stay and look after things. The law will be here for hours."

Tony comes over to us and asks Martin if he knows what his wife usually kept in the safe and Martin says she never kept much money and all the jewelry was paste. He can't remember just *what* was there, so Tony says that it's too bad. We go out in the hall and see the doctor and he says the maid's still scared but O.K. and Martin and I go to his office.

I figure I'm hard and all that but then I get a shock. Martin looks at his watch and says: "We better eat. We got just about time before we meet the gals."

I'm holding a highball glass and I drop it. I look at him and he gets red and says: "Why not! I didn't kill her and I wasn't in love with her at any time."

I get thinking then. I've had a dirty little hunch for the last hour. We talk a little bit more and take another drink and before we start out to eat I say: "If I was you I'd see my lawyer tonight. You're liable to need him pretty bad tomorrow."

He looks dumb at me and I explain that the first thing the law looks for is motive and that this killing is senseless for a burglar. I tell him he's the logical suspect and that he'd probably be in jail now if it hadn't been that Mac and Tony knew me and believed me. He says: "I haven't any motive."

I say: "You'll get her money."

Then I get another shock. He says:

"She left most of her money to two colleges and what's left goes to the Community Relief Fund. She was very charitable."

This knocks the motive stuff all to hell. I'd remembered the funny way he'd looked when he saw the safe was open, and this wanting to step out the same night his wife was killed had made me think he'd had her killed. It was just a hunch though. He says: "She told me that about a month ago and showed me the will."

I think this over and decide I'm wrong. I say:

"If *you're* not worried *I'm* certainly not," and we go out and eat.

We go on the party though I don't want to, and I see that he don't stay late or get stiff. There's decency in all things and I still got a little even if I am a private copper.

Instead of going back to the house we go to a hotel that night. Adjoining rooms. It's about one-thirty when we check in and can't sleep from thinking about all that's happened and about how Mrs. Martin looked on that door. About two I think I hear somebody talking in Martin's room. I slip out of bed and try to hear through the wall and can't and then I go into the closet which has thinner walls and I hear him say:

"Right away, then."

I can't tell where he's standing but I don't hear any other voices so I figure he's phoning. I get dressed and look out the window and see there's a ledge that runs from my window almost to his. I wait until I hear him open the door and hear a little talk that I can't understand and then I sneak my window open and climb out a little way on the ledge but I can't go far because there's nothing to hang on to after I get where I can't reach my window. I feel like a young robin just learning to fly out there and if it was daylight I'd probably look like one. Martin's got his window open though and I can hear all right and I can see one corner of his room, the corner that has the head of the bed.

THE FIRST thing I hear is Martin saying: "He's in the next room asleep. He's half drunk trying to keep me sober." Then I hear somebody else say: "I don't get the idea of coming up tonight."

Martin says: "I can't meet you tomorrow the time I said I would and I wanted to talk to you."

The other guy says: "Why not?"

This one's got a slow, sleepy way of talking that rings a bell someplace in my head but not strong enough to place him. Martin says: "I've got to attend that inquest in the morning. This didn't work out so good. Cass says the law knows it's murder and figures I'm in it."

Soft talk says: "And then what?"

Martin tells him: "If it hadn't been you broke into the safe it'd been just too bad for me. The way it is, they'll figure she came in in the middle of a robbery and got killed to shut her mouth."

Soft talk laughs very quietly and says: "That was an idea."

Martin acts like he's about half sore. He says: "It worked out all right, but I don't get the idea. There wasn't anything in there that was worth a damn."

The other guy laughs again and says: "It'll be two grand now for services rendered and another two grand for tearing up what wasn't worth a damn." He's laughing at Martin on this last.

Martin says: "What you mean?" then, and the other guy says: "Don't play dumb!" and they both shut up for a minute. Then Martin says: "O.K., I'll pay it."

I hear somebody walking and the other fella comes over and sits on the bed where I can see him. It's Tod Debenham. By this time I'm so damn' mad I can hardly hold on to the window and stay on my corner of the ledge, I'd forgotten all about seeing Debenham by Martin's house in the excitement, and with what I hear it all falls into line. I've got the picture now!

I pull myself back into my own window but still listen, and I hear Martin say: "Then I'll see you at the Anchor Apartments as soon as I get through with the inquest and go to the bank."

Debenham says something I can't hear and Martin tells him: "I'll see that I'm not followed. And I'll see that Cass isn't with me." Then he lowers his voice a little and I can't hear anything plain until I hear the door of his room open and close.

By this time I know how I'm going to work it. If I go out and pick Debenham as he goes out of the room I'll not get to first base. This Debenham is from down south some place, comes from a good family, but is just a killer by heart. He's the kind of a dude that bucks the law for excitement. If he was an ordinary hood I'd pick him and let the cops find out what they want to know with a rubber hose, but I've got Debenham picked as the kind that'd be beat to death before he'd open his face. The old southern gentleman instinct, or whatever it is. All I can do is play along and get him and Martin together with proof. If I accuse Martin of hiring Debenham to kill his wife I've got nothing to show for it except hearing some talk that doesn't prove anything and that he can deny. I think over what I'm going to do and go back to bed.

In the morning, when we go to the inquest, I get McAndrews to one side and tell him about it. He gets hold of the coroner before the thing starts and it goes over very smooth. The coroner steers away from any questions that Martin might have trouble in answering and the verdict is, "Death by a person or persons unknown." As soon as this is over Martin takes me to one side and says he's got business that he'll have to do by himself. He winks at me to give me an idea it's monkey business. He says he'll meet me at four at his office. It's 11:30 now. I say: "O.K.," and he beats it, and McAndrews and Corte come over and tell me they've decided to stick around with me and be in at the finish, if there is one.

I'm beating it for a phone and I tell them on the way there that if they want to follow me and stick fairly close it's dice, but that if they stick too close it's no dice. I finally get it through their heads that Debenham is smart and that one man has a chance of getting action where three wouldn't. I tell 'em to beat it down to this Anchor Apartment place which is on West Sixth Street, and when they see me go in to wait about five minutes and follow me in but to keep out of sight before then because Debenham may be watching. This finally sticks after an argument.

I call up a little rat pool hustler that works for me then. This little guy is plenty smart some ways but a chump some others but he's a swell tag because he looks harmless, I tell him where to meet me and go out and grab a hack.

I PICK this hustler, Arlie Epstein his name is, up on the corner of Sixth and Hill and we go out Sixth until about a block from where this Anchor dive is. We get out then and I tell Arlie what to do and he goes on the same side of the street the apartment is on, and I pull my hat down and go down the other and pray every foot of the way that Debenham don't see me. It's the weak point of the scheme. I duck into a grocery store that some Greek boy is running right across from the apartment. It's about 12:30 then.

The Greek comes over, and I buy an apple and stall around eating it, and nothing happens. Arlie's hanging around the front of the Anchor and that's all. I've got to eat three more apples before Martin shows up and I don't like apples. He comes in a cab and stops in front of the apartment. The minute he goes in I step out far enough in the doorway of the grocery store so that Arlie can see me and he follows Martin in.

He sticks his head out the door in a couple of minutes and makes motions and I go over. Arlie says: "Six-A. Right down the hall on the right."

I say: "O.K., Arlie. Here's the ten now in case I don't see you. You stick here and if there's a battle and two cops come rushing in you tell 'em where I'm at." He nods his head and I go in the apartment house.

It's one of these fakes that have a desk but nobody behind it. The whole place looks like a vacuum cleaner would do it a lot of good and I can tell somebody's been cooking cabbage. I go down the hall trying to figure what I'm going to do next but it turns out I don't have a worry. Martin's only been in the place about five minutes and I don't think he's had time to get through with his business, but when I get to Six-A I hear somebody start to open the door.

The halls are about ten feet wide and straight as a string. I couldn't duck if I wanted to. I stand there and get a gun out from under my coat. The door opens wide and I see Martin's back in the door and hear him say: "I'll be see—"

I see a strange face over Martin's shoulder and I see it change when the guy sees me. It sort of tightens up and then I brace myself and go in. I've done a little wrestling and I know this shoulder butt business and how it should be done, so I get one foot against the wall to start me off and take a dive clear of the floor and hit Martin in the back and just above the hips with my shoulder. It knocks him ahead and off his feet and into the guy in front of him so hard he falls on top of him. I've hit him so hard I keep going and I take the fall on my right shoulder and do a half twist so I'm facing the room and laying on my right side.

Debenham's across the room from me, just getting out of a chair. He's stooping a little, the way he would be, and grabbing at his coat pocket. I've still kept my gun during the acrobatics, and I shoot once and it straightens him up with the back of his knees against the front of his chair. While he straightens he gets the gun out of his pocket and I don't take any chances but pop him again and this one sets him back in the chair like he was thrown there. He ain't over ten feet from me and a .45 will hit an awful smack at a distance like that. I know he's out for good, for all and forever.

I look at the tangle Martin and the other guy are in then. I've rolled maybe six feet in front of them and am still laying on the floor like they are. I see Martin start to disentangle himself, and I get up and clip him across the face with the barrel of my gun, and I clip hard. I hear it crunch. He flops down again on the other boy and if it *had* been a wrestling match it'd been called a body press and he'd have got a fall. He just smothers the other guy.

I yank him off and look at what's under him. The guy is damn' near smothered and still don't know what it's all about. He looks up and sees my gun pointed at him and don't even move until I tell him to. I back him to a wall and make him face it and take a gun away from him and then make him turn around and sit with his back to the wall. Martin's out and will be for at least an hour and Debenham's out forever, and I figure that if I talk fast I might be able to learn something before Mac and Tony bust in. I do but not much, I don't have time.

Mac and Tony come boiling in carrying guns out and ready, like they expected to fight an army, and right along with 'em is Arlie. Mac takes in the lay-out quick, goes over to Debenham and looks at him and then he says: "Very nice, Johnny. You caught him right in the adam's apple."

I see Arlie with his mouth open so damn' far I can see where his adam's apple ought to be, and I tell him: "Beat it, Arlie," and he does. Then I say to Mac: "Why not take Martin and this heel up to the station and see what they know. Martin's just bought a will his wife left in the safe that was robbed. He paid two grand for it, and paid another two grand to the guys that killed her for him. This heel claims he didn't have anything to do with the killing, but he's already said that he's the one that gagged Martin's maid and a charge of attempted murder ought to fix him up. I wink at Mac and Mac gets it and says: "We can charge him with it anyway, but hell! Why not stick him on the murder rap. I can pin it on him just like a false front."

The guy breaks right then. He's a yellow pup and I know he will. He spills the whole thing before even the ambulance and the fast wagons get there that Mac has sent for, and he pulls the rope tighter around Martin's neck with every word.

IN THE first place Martin tries to hire him to kill his wife. The guy won't go for that. Then Martin hires him to hide in his closet and pretend to sap him. This was so I wouldn't get wise that Martin wasn't right. He wanted me to be with him all the time, on account of being an alibi, and he figured that if I thought he was in danger from his wife I'd stick. Then Martin hires Debenham to kill his wife and gets this guy to go along with him and help take care of the interference, if any. Debenham'd kill his *own* wife for two hundred dollars and Martin offers him two thousand. The rest is just like I figured it.

This guy—his name is Albert Hood, though he ain't got guts enough to be one—goes to the house about an hour before we're due home. They knock on the back door and tie up and gag the cook and sap the butler when he comes out in the kitchen. Then they go upstairs and Debenham goes to Mrs. Martin's room while this guy looks for the maid. He's the kind that *would* be brave around women. He admits gagging the girl but claims that when he went in the bedroom Debenham already had Mrs. Martin hanging on the door and was working on the safe. It don't make any difference. He's talked himself into an accessory charge and is too dumb to know it.

About this time the ambulance and the fast cars from the station come and the doctor patches Martin's face, where I slugged him, up enough to take him to the station.

He hasn't come to yet and the doctor says he won't for quite a while longer. Mac and Tony load Martin and this fella Hood into one of the cars to take 'em up and book 'em, and then I remember something. I say to Mac: "Hey! Wait a minute! This Martin owes me for two days work on this week. What about it?"

Mac gives me that dirty grin he's got and says: "You should have collected before you had him arrested. I bet he'll be mad at you now and *never* pay you."

He never did, either.

DICE AND NO DICE

IT LOOKED LIKE NO DICE WHEN NIGGER EISMAN TURNED UP WITH A PERFECT ALIBI FOR THE CULLEN KILLING. BUT THE KILLER HAD WALKED OUT WITH SEVENTEEN HUNDRED AND FIFTY DOLLARS THAT BELONGED TO DETECTIVE JOHNNY CASS, AND WHEN EISMAN TURNED UP WITH A COUPLE OF SNAKE-EYES JOHNNY FIGURED IT WAS TIME TO PICK UP THE IVORIES AND ROLL AGAIN.

IT'S **A** honey of a crap game… for Farmer Sheats that's running it. I drop a hundred and twenty but I ain't crying about it because if I'd got over I'd have got a cut of between five and six grand as near as I can count. There's about that much in it. I've just lost the dice and the hundred and twenty and am standing right back of George Cullen that's got the dice now, and Nigger Eisman is right next to George waiting for 'em. George is rattling the dice in his hand and has got five twenties laying in front of him that's taken, but he's holding tight so's to give the side-bettors a chance to get their dough on the line.

Half of these are calling for how much they think he'll make his point, which happens to be eight, and the other half of 'em are saying for how much he'll seven and it's the usual madhouse that a big crap game always is.

MICKEY CATARINA'S taking the cut for the house and the game's big enough so Farmer's watching him which isn't usual. Mickey reaches out and takes a fin for the house and says: "Hit the board, George!"

George nods and says: "Eight just once, dice!" and draws his arm back to bounce 'em against the back of the table.

Just then Nigger grabs his arm and says: "No dice!"

He holds George's hand and says to Mickey: "These are bum dice. He can't seven with 'em."

Mickey says, "Gimme!" and holds out his hand for the dice. George gives 'em to him and says, "Look good, Mickey!" and turns and takes Nigger right in the puss.

He's all braced and set and he times it perfect. Nigger can't fall backward because there's too many people behind him and they keep him from going that way, but he bounces on them and then just sort of slips to the floor and lands on his back. George takes a step ahead and holds his foot about a foot above Nigger's face and then stamps down with it—but Nigger don't know it.

I grab George before he works on him any more, not because I give a damn about Nigger but because I don't want George going up on a murder rap.

Farmer's seen the whole thing. He goes over to Mickey and looks the dice over and tosses them on the board. They show seven which proves Nigger was wrong about them being crooked dice. He says to Mickey: "How much did Nigger drop?"

And when Mickey says, "Not over fifty bucks!" he says, "Pick him up."

There's a guy waiting to go on shift in Mickey's place that I don't know and he and some guy that Nigger fell against pick him up, and they and Farmer go into the washroom and I go along with 'em for two reasons: I want to hear Farmer tell Nigger what the score is because I don't like him five cents' worth; and I'm now out of money and figure I'll get a hundred off Farmer and get back in the game. I figure a hundred more won't hurt me too much and there's percentage in that big a game if you can ever get over.

They throw water in his face and Farmer and I stand there waiting for him to come to. He's got on a new suit

This guy looks us over and
pops George Cullen.

that's a light flashy gray, and when George stepped on his face it busted his nose and he's bled all over the front of it. He's a mess.

He comes around finally and looks up at us groggy as hell, and Farmer says: "Here's the lousy fifty you lost and if you ever come in my place again I'll not only throw you out but I'll see you'll get a floater out of town from then on. Get that, Nigger?"

Farmer's got enough drag to do just that little thing and Nigger knows it. He gets up shaky as hell and takes the money and then says, "All right, Farmer!" and wobbles through the door. Farmer says to the house man: "See that he gets as far as the steps, Sam, and—" He winks and Sam, who's a big husky bird, winks back and they go out.

Farmer don't even ask me what I want; which proves how smart he is but just says: "How much, Johnny?"

I say: "A hundred'll do. I can't be sick always."

He gives me the hundred and I go back and get in the game.

AN HOUR later I'm well again. I've run the hundred up to about seventeen-fifty and I've got the dice and have just made my point and am going to try for a seven when somebody says: "Heist 'em, boys."

I look up, see two masked guys, one standing right by the door where he's got the room under control, the other by the side. The first guy's got two guns and the second, one. The door's about thirty feet from me and I think fast.

I've got two-fifty on the table and the rest of it, fifteen hundred, in my left hand, and I figure I can toss this under the table as I raise my hands and as soon as the heist guys are gone I can find it.

I do this.

There's a little guy wedged in next to me that's been rattling about ten dollars in silver in his hand and betting dollars against points. He sees me toss my fifteen hundred under the table and I'm damned if he don't throw his ten in silver after it! When the silver hits the floor it sounds as loud as an automobile smash-up.

Nobody could miss it and the guy at the door don't. He says: "Line up against the wall and face it!" and waves his guns and we do just what we're told. Then he says to his partner: "Shake 'em down, keed! The cash drawer is on the far side and there's money under the table."

Keed goes through the crowd and cleans us right down to and including carfare, and takes the money out of the house drawer and dives under the table, and I can hear him grunt when he finds my roll. He even gets the guy's silver that he was so proud of.

Then the guy by the door says to us: "Turn around."

We do. I'm so mad I can hardly see, not so much at the heist guys as at the little dope that pitched the chicken-feed, but what happens next scares the mad out of me. We're all lined up against the wall, maybe twenty, maybe twenty-five of us, and this guy looks us over and comes up with his right-hand gun and pops George Cullen, who's standing right by me. When he does I see the gray coat he's wearing and it's the same one Nigger had on. There's blood down the front of it just the same way and it's cut the same and made out of the same flashy cloth.

I get all this in the second it takes George to fall forward on his face.

The guy waves his guns and says, "Don't hurry!" to us and to his partner, "Le's go, keed!" Keed goes out the door and the trigger man follows him out backward and we just stand there and watch 'em go. The game's really a hustler's game and all these boys know enough not to run after a guy with a gun. They figure all they lost is money and I figure the same way right along with 'em. We couldn't stop the guys and all we'd do is take chances on being laid on a slab alongside of Cullen.

I know he's dead but I squat by him and see I'm right. Farmer goes ever and locks the door and calls out: "As soon as the law comes you boys can go but I don't want any questions about what's happened. There'll be no beef. Get the time straight and remember what's happened as plain as you can because you're going to be witnesses in a murder trial."

He comes over to me and squats down alongside and says: "Dead?"

"Plenty," I say.

He says, "You know who don't you?" and I say: "Nigger Eisman. I'll call MacAndrews at the station if you want, Farmer. He'll give you as much of a break as any of 'em and maybe more."

"Go ahead," he says.

We got to call the law because the room's so sound-proof nobody could have heard the shot unless they was right against the door. I go over to the phone then and call the station and get homicide and ask for MacAndrews, and he's in which is a break. I tell him it's me—Johnny Cass—and where I am and what's happened and for him to come down, and then I say: "It'll save time if you put out a pick-up on Nigger Eisman. He's the guy that done it."

He says: "It's easy done if I want to but why should I?"

I say: "He's the one that done it, I tell you. There's at least twenty witnesses."

"How long ago did this happen?" he says.

I LOOK at my watch and see it's 11:26 and I know this happened at 11:23 because I looked at the time then in case of any question.

"Three minutes ago," I say.

He says: "Eisman's been here for at least twenty minutes talking to Tony and me. He's damn near drove us nuts trying to get us to put in a good word for him with Farmer so Farmer won't put the bee on him in all the rest of the joints."

"What kind of a coat's he got on?" I say.

I hear MacAndrews talk to somebody else in the homicide room and then he says: "He's got on a gray coat. He's got a smashed schnozzle and it's bled all over the front of it."

I say: "Well, come on down!" and hang up the phone and tell Farmer what he said.

Farmer's place is on Spring and not over eight blocks from the station. It takes Mac about five minutes to make it and he knocks on the door and Farmer lets him and Tony Carte, his partner in, and they've brought Eisman with 'em.

This Eisman is only called Nigger because he's got thick fat lips and is dark. And he's just one of those dirty stinking kind of two-bit hustlers that hang around the real ones. He comes in, feeling plenty snotty, and looks at me and Farmer and says: "Trying to hang this on me, hunh. It's no dice because I was at the station when it happened and I can't be framed."

He's just as smart about it as he can well be. Farmer looks at me and shakes his head so I don't say anything. By the time Mac and Tony take everybody's names and where they live there's a photographer there and about twenty other cops, some in uniform and some not, and an assistant district attorney and the place is jammed.

Farmer's got this D.A. over to one side and is talking to beat hell and then Mac calls out: "You can all go home but don't leave town without coming up to the station and telling me. You're material witnesses and I don't want to have to go after you." He knows he's safe in letting 'em go like that because they're mostly birds that live without working and can't afford to jam with the law over anything like being witnesses.

I start to go with 'em but Farmer sings out, "Wait, Johnny!" so I do. He gets through with the D.A. and gets his hat and I say goodnight to Mac and Tony and we start to go. I say, "Where?" and he says: "Le's go to Herbert's and talk it over."

So we get a hack in front and go there and sit at a table and order and then Farmer says: "And what d'ya think of it?"

I've done plenty of thinking. Whoever done it got away with seventeen hundred and fifty dollars of my money and this hurts. I don't like to have George Cullen killed right alongside of me but after all he's no particular friend of mine and this don't bother me as much as losing the dough does.

"Why in hell should Nigger start the beef with George?" I say. "That was a phony. He'd lost fifty slugs but what of that. That wouldn't start him out unless he was higher than a kite and he didn't act like it."

Farmer asks: "Does he use the weed?" and I say: "Sure! But he didn't act like he was high tonight."

"You want to work on it for me, Johnny?" Farmer says.

I say: "Yes, you bet. I'm going to do seventeen hundred and fifty dollars' worth of work on it for my own side."

He says: "The D.A.'s going to act as if it was a row in a private club so I won't get jammed for running a spot, but I had between four and five grand in that drawer. If I hadn't got a break I'd have had to pay out every one of the customers on a frequenting-a-gambling-house rap. I'm out and injured."

"You ain't got any cherry," I say. "I'll scout around and see what I can see."

He thinks about this for a while and says: "Cullen was in this, it's a gut. If Eisman's row with him was to make it look good for the shooting later on, which I think and you think, he must be. How's that for an angle?"

I tell him that it's maybe O.K. and we go. He's got to cash a check to pay our ticket. He's cleaned out as pretty as I am.

I FIGURE Farmer's got a good idea about Cullen but that I've got a better one. MacAndrews and Corte think we was seeing things when we saw Nigger Eisman but I know better. If Nigger had an alibi, and he's got a cast-iron one, somebody else didn't know he was going to have and was going to use him for the goat—whoever did the job. That's first-grade stuff. Also they wouldn't know he had blood all over the front of his coat unless they had seen him in the hour between the time of the beef with Cullen and the time of the heist. That's second-grade. Also Eisman wouldn't have picked a beef with Cullen unless he was in the dope some way. That's third-grade only it'd be eighth if I could figure why he'd spot himself as a killer, and then back out on it.

The fourth-grade is a lot harder. I scout around a little that night and don't do any good and it's around three the next afternoon before I find out where Eisman lives… the Continental Hotel on South Main.

I beat it right down there and Eisman ain't in when I get there but comes in while I'm asking the clerk what room he's got. He sees me and starts to back out but he ain't got a chance because I see him at the same time he sees me. I grab him and say: "Le's go in your room and talk," and he stalls a little but we go back.

Just as soon as we get inside I shut the door and tell him to sit down and then I see he's higher'n a kite. He's got that dopey, screwy expression that shows it all over his face… a kind of silly grin that tells the score right down to runs, hits and errors.

"High, hunh!" I say; and he looks at me and grins and says: "Uh-huh."

I tell him that he's behind the eight ball and he tells me I'm crazy. Then he starts to tell me why I am. He's just so damn high he's got to brag to somebody and I'm there.

"You know Felix Ullman's place?" he says.

I do and I say so. Felix runs a cigar stand and is fronting for some bird that's making book in the back room of the spot. He goes on with: "Well, I was there yesterday about noon putting five on Jackie Horner's nose in the fourth at Caliente." He swears some here at somebody that touted Jackie Homer to him. "The dog thought he was the little lamb and the rest of the field was Mary. He'd have come in tenth except there was only nine horses running."

He's so dinged up that I figure it's better to let him go and not try to hurry him. I lost five myself on Jackie Horner to place and I know how he feels when it comes right down to it. He says: "While I was in there some guy comes over to me and says do I want to make fifty smackers. I say yes and he takes me over to one side and says it's mine if I pick a beef with George Cullen and let him take me." He kind of puffs up on this and explains that that's the only reason he lets George take him. In the shape he's in he even believes it.

"Who was this guy?" I say; and he says: "I don't know him but I've seen him in there once or twice before. He comes in there always with some other guy and this other guy calls him Oley."

I ask him what he looks like and he says: "He's about as tall as I am but he's got a big belly. He's bald as an egg on top of his head and just got a fringe around the edges and is light-complected." He goes on then with: "I tell him I'll do it and he says he'll pay me when I do. I back up on it then and he gives me twenty of it then and is going to give me the rest later."

"You think you'll get it?" I say.

"I know I will!" he says, and takes out a sweetheart of a stop watch that's worth half a grand of anybody's money. He shows it to me and explains: "He give this to me to hold and is going to meet me here with the other thirty at five today to get it out of soak." He nods his head at me as if that should show me what a smart dope he is.

I look at my watch and see it's ten to four. I say: "Where did you see him after you left the joint?" and he says: "In the cafeteria up the street from there. He and his friend were there waiting for me to see whether I did it or not. As soon as I talk to them I figure it's maybe a phony so I go up to the station and make myself an out. I guess I'm half smart."

I don't know whether he'll remember what he's told me when the marijuana wears off but I hope he does. I figure to ask him then how smart he is. He hasn't got any phone in his room and I figure that maybe the guy that did the job *will* take a chance and come in and pay off because they won't know I know anything about the set-up, and may figure that it's safer to pay Eisman so he'll keep his mouth shut. It'd be a sucker stunt but the whole thing's so screwy I figure it's a good bet.

"I'm going out," I say to Eisman. "Be right back."

He goggles at me and pulls out another reefer and grins at me and says: "I'll be right here when you get back."

He is….

I'VE GONE to the lobby and telephoned. I get Mac and tell him to come on down if he wants to make the pinch and he says he will and I go back to the room. I knock on the door and Nigger don't say anything and I try the knob and it's locked. I pound some more thinking he's passed out. He was so damn high I don't think he can walk out and he didn't act like he wanted to take a powder on me.

About then my foot slips in something on the floor. I look down and see a dark spot that gets bigger while I look at it and right then I get the smell of fresh blood. There's no mistake if you ever smell it once. I get back against the wall across the hall and slam into the door with my shoulder, and this breaks the lock and I fall over Eisman.

He's laying on his back about a foot from the door when it's open, and somebody has fixed him up good. Really first-class. There's a spot on his temple that means he got clouted there and then somebody's taken a knife and just ripped his neck open. This has cut the big artery and he's bled to death while he was knocked cold and this means plenty of blood.

For a minute it gets me. The phone booth's at the side of the lobby and all the time I telephoned Mac I kept watch, and I know nobody either went back or come out through the hall. I know it can't be suicide because marijuana smokers don't do the dutch hardly ever for one thing, and he wasn't even feeling low for another, and what makes it murder for sure is that there's no knife. I look.

I sit down on the bed and try and figure it out, and here's a closet with the door standing open and that tells the story. Whoever did the killing was in the room when Nigger and I come down the hall, and he heard us and hid there and heard Nigger tell the story of his life to me and figured that with Nigger dead things'd shape up better, and come out and smacked him when I left and made sure he was dead by cutting his throat. This makes it look like the bird that Nigger alibied for must be it, and it makes any chance of me tagging him at Ullman's no dice, because he's heard Nigger tell me about him hanging around there and'll give the place a miss from now on. The whole thing don't look so good.

I sit there and watch these puffy lips of Eisman's change color and think this all out before Mac comes. He sneaks down the hall and knocks real quiet and I whisper just loud enough so's he can hear it: "Come in!" He does, very quiet, looking at me instead of at his feet—and falls over the body and goes on his face.

Then he gets up and I say: "Meet the boy friend!" and I wave at Nigger.

He looks at him and says: "Did you have to—" then sees how his neck is chopped up and changes it to: "Who done it?"

I tell him that I don't know and this makes him sore and he says: "You was here, wasn't you?"

Mac's like that, flies off the handle easy. He says: "What was the idea in getting me in here and making me fall over it?" He waves at the body.

I say: "It was your own feet you fell over." It burns him up but he lets it slide. I tell him how it happened and that the guy locked the door after himself and must have gone out the back way and about what Nigger told me about this Oley, whoever he is.

"Ullman might know," Mac says then.

I say: "He *might!*" and Mac says: "He better."

He calls the morgue wagon and the print man and all the rest of the staff at the station and I beat it. I know Ullman and I don't think Ullman's going to know a thing that he'll talk about. Mac could take some guy that didn't know the score too well down to the station and make him think up stories if he didn't know any, but this Ullman'll know what Mac can and can't do. He's got plenty of protection on his joint or he wouldn't be running the way he is, and a guy like that's got too many connections to get rough with just on a guess. As soon as Mac gets down to earth he'll figure the same way and I know it so I can't see any sense in wasting time sticking along with him.

I START right then on Farmer Sheats' hunch because it's all I got left, and make the rounds of the joints trying to find somebody that knows something about Cullen. The catch on this is everybody knew him and don't know anything about him. He was one of these birds that don't get up until the joints open and stays until they close and that don't seem to have any home. It takes me three days before I get a lead, but when I do I find out he's married and has got a kid and lives out in the Wilshire district which is a damn nice neighborhood.

I go out there and find his apartment and knock on the door and a little short dark woman comes to the door and I say: "Mrs. Cullen?"

She says she is and looks scared to death. I say: "I want to talk to you," and she says: "Won't you come in?"

I do. They got a pip of an apartment, the kind that rents for at least a hundred and fifty, and this is important money for a hustler to be paying for rent. She waves me to a chair and says in this scared way: "George isn't home, officer. I don't know where he is."

She's got me picked as a copper which is all right with me for a while. If I figure I can get more out of her by telling her I run a private agency there's always time. I never think about her maybe not knowing what the score is and say: "Why, didn't you know George was dead?"

It's a hell of a thing to do but I don't think. She looks at me like she don't understand and says: "What did you say?" and then sees by my face that she's heard right. She looks at me for a minute and then says, "Oley!" as if to herself and starts to cry.

I let her go for a minute and think what a heel I am to tell her like that and she says, still crying: "George knew it. He knew it was going to happen."

I say: "He had a hunch?" and she says: "He told me we were going to move away from here because he was afraid of Oley."

I say: "Oley who?" and she says: "Oley Chrisman." She's really going to town with her crying and it's like talking to somebody who's answering questions they don't know is being asked 'em. Like somebody talking in their sleep. I say: "What made him think that?" and she says: "He and George quarreled something terrible the last time he was here. Oley's brother was quarreling with George too."

I say: "What about?"

She keeps on crying and mumbles: "I don't know!" and I say: "George is dead, Mrs. Cullen. Anything you tell me may help me find the man that killed him." She cries harder than ever and says: "It was my fault. The whole thing was my fault. If I only hadn't asked George to quit."

"Quit what?" I say.

She looks up at me and says: "Kidnaping!"

I stare at her and she says: "George and Oley and his brother and a woman Oley said was his wife, only I don't think she was, were kidnaping people. I made George tell them he was going to stop it."

I've changed my mind about it being such a raw stunt telling her about her old man. If she had a chance to think it over she wouldn't be talking like this. She's lived with a hustler and if she wasn't about half nuts she'd clam up like one. I got her at just the right time.

"Did you ever hear any names?" I say.

She says: "I heard the name McClure once. And Sullivan. I heard that too. That was when they were all arguing, the night before George went away." She puts her head down on her hands and really goes to town again with her crying on this and I let her go because I got to have a minute to think.

For the last six months there's been talk around the joints about some snatch gang that works the big hotels for married men that want to party a bit. They let him meet some gal and seem to get over with her pretty well and when she takes him to her apartment they bust in and take him. The gal's supposed to be a respectable married woman just out for no good and the guy can't squawk on her account as well as his own. He'd have to admit being where he shouldn't. There's never been a beef come out yet because this bunch is smart enough to put the slug on easy—maybe five, never over ten grand—and give the sap plenty of time to raise it. A guy won't cry on a touch like that where he would if it was lots of money. I don't remember either the name McClure or Sullivan but I think of another way to check on it.

"How long have you lived here, Mrs. Cullen?" I say.

"About six months," she says. "We came from Kansas City. George got in some trouble there and...."

This fits fine. I can't see why George and his friends have a beef about him quitting though, so I say: "Why did you want him to stop?"

"This woman that was supposed to be Oley's wife," she says, "was always making eyes at George!" She breaks down here and starts in to cry good again and sobs out: "He got killed just because I was jealous of him."

I SMOOTH her down a little and wonder a guy that was as smart as this George Cullen must have been should have married a half-wit of a woman. He might have quit the other boys because she wanted him to but they didn't knock him off on account of that. I think of another way to check this kidnap yarn and ask her where the phone is and she points it out to me. I call the station and get Mac.

"Mac," I say, "did you ever hear of anyone named McClure and Sullivan?"

He speaks back real quick. He says: "McClure was picked up in a ditch last week but wasn't identified till this morning. Why?"

"I just wondered," I say. "What about Sullivan?"

He says: "Never heard the name. What about McClure? Why did you ask?"

I say: "Nevermind. I'll tell you when I see you," and hang up the phone and go back to the woman. I ask her if she has any idea where this Oley Chrisman hangs out and she says she don't and then I figure I'll check on Nigger's description and I say: "He's blond, ain't he?"

"Why no," she says. "He's dark and he's got curly black hair parted in the middle. He's heavy." I ask her how tall and she shows me about five feet and a half high in the air.

I got another hunch now so I say: "You better get in touch with the law, Mrs. Cullen. I'm only a private detective!" And I get out while she stares.

I get down to the front of the apartment house and just as I step out on the street I hear a siren howl and along comes Mac and Tony Corte in a fast wagon. Mac sees me and climbs out and says: "What's this about McClure?"

His face is red and I can see he's so damn mad he can't hardly talk. It burns him up to think I'm holding out on anything he should have found out by himself. It takes me about ten minutes to tell him what the gal told me and then he says: "And you don't know where this Chrisman is?" and looks at me like he don't believe it.

I say: "I don't. There's two Oley Chrismans. One blond and bald-headed and the other dark and with black curly hair. As soon as I find more of them I'm going to put 'em with the Smiths in the phone book."

He says: "And you don't know where to find 'em, hunh?"

I say: "No. Believe it or not."

"For two cents," he says, "I'd stick around with you for a while." I give him a nickel and tell him that he owes me three cents and he says: "You mick! You hold out on me and you'll wish you hadn't."

I say: "Come along then."

He stares at me as mean as he can and says: "I know you're holding out on me. That's why I traced the telephone call."

"So what?" I say.

He says to Corte: "Come on, Tony. Le's go up and see what this woman's got to say."

They go into the apartment house and I head for a phone booth.

I start calling up hotels and make it on the fifth one. The Belvedere. A nice place. I say: "Have you had a Mr. Sullivan registered at your hotel in the last week or two that went away without his luggage?" I know that if anybody does a stunt like that it makes talk among the help.

The girl says: "Wait a minute!" and I wait and by and by she says: "Hello. Who is this speaking?"

"Missing Persons," I say, which is taking an awful chance if the hotel has reported it to Missing Persons. But in a minute a man says: "This is Mr. Fields, the manager. You were asking about Mr. Arthur Sullivan?" I say: "Yes."

I hear him talk to somebody else and then he says: "Can you come down here? It's very important."

I've started something I don't know what to do with. Then I think that even if worse comes to worse and there's trouble I can always say they misunderstood on the Missing Persons gag and that I can't be stuck for impersonating an officer on that kind of proof so I start. There's something doing and I want to know what.

I GO into the lobby and ask for this Mr. Fields and he's left word for me because a bell-boy takes me to his office plenty quick. This Fields is a thin, worried-looking bird and he doesn't look too happy when he says: "You're from Missing Persons?"

"I'm John Cass!" I say, and let him take the Missing Persons thing for granted.

"This is Mr. Zeil," he says, and waves at a little dark Jewish-looking guy and I shake hands with him not knowing what it's all about. This Zeil says: "Mr. Fields and I had just decided to call you."

I sit down and say nothing and Fields says: "We didn't know what to do. We were just talking when your call came."

I let Zeil tell the story and it's just what I thought it is. He and Sullivan run a real-estate office and a hotel in Santa Barbara and have quite a bit of property. Zeil gets a letter from Sullivan that tells him to dig up ten thousand in cash and to give this to a man that'll give him another letter from him. The pay-off is here at the Belvedere but Zeil gets thinking about it and don't believe the letter where it says it's for a business deal.

He explains: "We got spread out before the slump and are land poor. Sully'd know that I'd have a hard time to get the money and that we can't afford to go in to anything else."

He and Sullivan and this Fields have been friends for years and so he asks him about it and they just about decided it was a phony when I call. The baggage being left in the room is the tip-off to them, though they are sure that Sullivan wrote the letter.

I say: "Does it say when the man'll call for the money with the letter?"

Zeil gives me the letter and I see that he's supposed to wait at the hotel from Wednesday on and it's Friday now. I ask him about this and he says he's been waiting but the more he thought it over the more he thought he ought to do something. Then I tell them that I heard of a man named McClure who's just been found dead and Sullivan mentioned in the same way and ask 'em if they'll let me go on it my way, and we talk it over and finally decide what to do and how to do it, and Fields calls in the house dick and tells him he's to do what I tell him. Fields don't want any fuss in the hotel but I tell him that whether there is or not depends on how the play comes up and he has to stand for this.

The play comes up that same night and there's no fuss.

I'm in Fields' office and I hear the buzzer on his desk tick three times which means that somebody asks the clerk for Zeil and I drift out easy into the lobby.

There's a short, runty-looking bird standing by the desk. By and by Zeil comes downstairs and he and this guy talk a minute and then the guy gives Zeil a letter. Zeil reads it and goes over to the clerk and asks for the envelope he's checked in the hotel safe, and the clerk gives it to him and he gives it to the guy and then I step in.

I don't make a move before because the guy has to get the money before the case is air-tight. I tip the wink to the house dick and step alongside this bird and say: "Easy, guy. It's a pinch."

Cullen has been shot and Nigger Eisman has been stabbed and this McClure has been killed some way I don't know about and I ain't taking any chances. I got a gun in my coat pocket and I got about three inches of the end of it into this guy's ribs when I speak.

He turns and looks at me and says, "What for?" just as easy as hell and I say: "It's only kidnaping now. It'll be murder on top of it by and by."

He says nothing to this but shoves his shoulders up like it's no never minds to him, and the house man and I take him out the back way so's not to tip anybody off that might be waiting for him. The whole thing goes so smooth that nobody even guesses there's been a pinch made and there's at least fifty people milling around the lobby. As soon as we get him out of sight we shake him down and don't even find a gun. He's got this envelope that Zeil gave him though, and he's got a letter addressed to Victor Chrisman and this is a break.

I load him into a cab and take him to the station and into the homicide room and say to Mac: "Here's one of the guys!"

Mac don't waste any time in getting into action. I don't even have time to tell him I know the answer to what he wants to know. He comes right over to the runt and says: "Where d'ya live?"

The guy gives him a snotty look and says, "You guess!" and Mac smacks him across the puss and the guy hits the floor so hard he bounces. He's out cold.

"He lives on Redondo," I say. "I just brought him up to park him and see if you want to make this pinch with me." I show Mac the letter, which is a bill from a radio company, and Mac says to another copper that's there, "When he comes to, put him away!" and to Corte, "Come on, Tony!" and we go.

THIS HOUSE on Redondo is in the third block up from where the street-car line ends on Washington. It's a nice neighborhood, all little houses but modern and most of 'em built this Spanish style. Mac coasts the police car into the curb a half block down from the house and I say to him: "This is going to be tough."

He grunts and gets out and says, "Why?" and I say: "Because this guy is plenty tough and there's this poor devil of a Sullivan in there with him. We got to call our shots."

He grunts again and pays no attention and says to Corte: "You take the back, Tony. Cass and I'll go in the front way." He's sore as hell because he thinks I'm trying to tell him what to do and just starts out with his head down and never a thought in it, and I got to tag along or lose my place.

He gives Corte barely enough time to get to the back and pulls up on the front porch and pushes the doorbell. There's nothing happens for a minute, but from where I'm standing back of him I think I see a shade on one of the front windows flicker. There's no light showing any place in the house and Mac keeps his finger on the bell and half turns to me and says: "I guess we're too—"

He gets that far and the front door opens and somebody reaches out and clouts him on the side of the head. Mac don't even see what hits him. There's a street light on the corner but the porch is so dark I just get the flash of the gun the guy uses to clout with as it comes down and I'm looking right at it.

Mac goes down like it was an ax he was hit with instead of a gun and I go through the door in a dive at about where the guy's knees should be, figuring that if he's going to shoot I can maybe upset him before he does.

He don't shoot but hits down at me as I come in. He misses my head and just hits me on the back and this don't bother me none. What does bother me is that I miss his knees and sprawl out there on the floor and can't see or hear a thing. I'm afraid to move. The door is either on a spring or he gave it a pull as he dodges back because it's closed now.

I lay there on my belly and listen and all of a sudden I hear a grunt and he smacks down with the gun again, but it lands on my shoulder instead of my head which is a break again.

It's the last one I get. This bird acts like he can see in the dark. I'm stretched out there and I got a gun in my right hand and all of a sudden he piles on top of me and gets my right wrist in two hands and puts on a wristlock that's a honey. I got to drop the gun to break it and I do this, and he changes it into a hammerlock but don't get a chance to put on any pressure because I get my head down and roll ahead. We're all tangled up with him still holding my wrist with both his hands and I shout, "Corte!" just as loud as I can, and smack whoever's got me with my left—but I can't get any weight behind it because he's holding me off balance.

This is the first he knows there's anybody in the play but Mac and me. He puts a twist on my wrist and puts me down to my knees and then he must remember that I've dropped the gun I had, because he lifts me up and changes his hold into a whip wristlock and pitches me over against the wall. I land sitting down.

This is a mistake but I can see how he makes it. He's got his gun and thinks I ain't. I've lost one but I got another one and I yank it out I got to hold it in my left hand because my right's still numb, but at that I figure it's even.

I hear Tony Corte pounding away at the back door and have got time to try and figure what in hell's holding him back before this bird makes a move. When he does I *know* he can see in the dark. I'm just sitting there, afraid to move because he could hear me, and he shoots and I hear the slug chunk into the wall right by my head.

The flash of the gun is heading right at me and it about half blinds me, but I shoot right at it once and then once to each side and about a foot away from it. While I shoot I get up to my knees and the minute I'm done I throw myself as far to the side as I can, hoping he won't be able to hear it above the bong of the gun. But I get another bad break.

I land into a chair and the damn thing skids across the floor generating plenty of noise, and he turns loose again. I feel a kind of jar in my left shoulder and high up but it don't seem to hurt at the time. I shoot twice back and move about five feet to one side and this time I manage not to run into anything.

I hear a kind of thud and then a little scramble, but I'm afraid to try for it. I only got one shell left in my gun and I can't waste it. I can hear Corte pounding away on the back door and it sounds like he's got something to pound with finally.

I hear a kind of groan and then I think I hear something move on the floor. Just then Corte smashes through the back door and comes in through the kitchen and the damn fool's got a flashlight in his hand, and as he comes into the front room he turns it full on me!

I DUCK and the guy on the floor shoots but Corte has kept on swinging his light and just as the guy shoots the light hits him. He's on his knees and right in front of a door. Corte and I shoot at the same time and he goes backwards through the door. Corte starts after him and I say: "Hold it. Turn on the light first."

He uses the flash some more and finds the light switch by the front door and turns it on. Just then Mac starts to pound on the outside and he lets him in. We all three look, and see a pair of feet sticking out this other door. I pick up my gun that's still got shells in it and then we move sideways until we can see what belongs to the feet, and here's the guy laying on his back and all shot to hell. He's deader than last Christmas's goose.

We hear another noise in the room beyond and ease in there, and here's a guy on the bed with tape across his pan and both his hands and his feet tied with more of it. We cut him loose and pull the tape from his puss taking a bunch of whiskers along with it, and he looks at us and sees he's on the right side once again and passes out. Corte goes in the bathroom and gets some water and throws it on him, and we find a bottle of bum rye in the kitchen and give him a slug of that. He comes out of it far enough to even watch us shake the stiff down.

We figure right away the blond bald head and the black curly hair angle. He's in his curly hair make-up when we come in and when he fell his toupée fell off and shows his egg head. He's a little short guy but built as solid as a Shetland pony, and I'll be damned if I see how I made out with him as good as I did. If I hadn't been scared to death it'd just been too bad.

He's got one hole in his head and along the edge of the blood the dark stain he's put on his face has run. That makes the dark complexion the woman said he had. He's got another hole right center on his wishbone and there's two more besides this in him, one low and to the right in his side and another just ticking his left arm. I figure that Corte and I made the two center shots when the light was on him and the other two was what I was doing in the dark.

We look at my own shoulder and the slug's made a little groove about half an inch deep right on top. It don't hurt any until I look at it and then it hurts like hell because I think about it. It's bleeding some and there's some cotton in the bathroom and we put some of this on it and tape it there. Then Corte goes out front to where all the neighborhood is flocked in the street and borrows a phone and calls the morgue wagon.

We load Sullivan in the car when the morgue wagon and medical examiner get there, and take him back to the station and sit him down in the homicide room. He tells us that the reason George Cullen falls out with his Swede pals was because after this guy McClure paid off they killed him and Cullen wouldn't go for that. This makes more sense than his wife's yarn about quitting because of her being jealous of him, though he probably told her that to keep peace in the family. McClure was still there the first day Sullivan was brought in and he knows McClure paid off and hears Chrisman and his brother tell Cullen they were afraid McClure would squawk.

We get a description of the woman, Chrisman's wife, from Sullivan and Mac puts out a pick-up for her, though it probably won't ever do any good. Then we go to Chrisman's cell and tell him we got brother put away on ice and that all he's got to do is sign the complaint; and I'll be damned if he don't look stubborn and say: "I'd really rather not."

We tell him we know what the score is and can prove it's a blackmail proposition along with the snatch and all that but he says that he could never make his wife see that and so he'd rather not.

Mac's just about ready to blow his cork on that, because he ain't got any proof on the McClure killing without it, and the kidnap rap won't stick either unless Sullivan beefs, but I get an idea. I go back to Sullivan.

I say: "Did you have a stop watch?"

We've searched the stiff but he didn't have any watch on him.

This Sullivan says: "Why no, but McClure did. I saw it and heard Chrisman and his brother talking about it. The brother you got in jail got it."

I say: "If we find that watch and ask you to testify to this will you do it? The gal angle won't come into it if you're only a witness like that."

He thinks a minute and says he will if we'll keep him in the clear and then he says: "But what's the watch got to do with it?"

Even Mac don't get it and I've told him where I saw the watch. So I explain: "If it can be proved that the brother we got in jail had it instead of the brother we killed, I say, *This* brother can be stuck for the Nigger Eisman killing. It don't make any difference who he's charged with killing as long as it sticks. He can only hang once."

Mac says: "We never took time to look but they'd shake him down before they'd put him away. It'll be on his property slip if he's got it. It'll be his neck if he has."

He rings a buzzer and when the clerk comes in he says: "Get me this fella Chrisman's property slip."

The clerk goes out and Mac says to me: "If he's only got it!" and then the clerk comes back with the slip.

We look and he has. Also he's got seventeen hundred and fifty that I get, which makes the difference between dice and no dice to me. Where Chrisman goes he ain't got no use for money.

THE JADE BEAST

"THE GREEKS MAY HAVE A WORD
FOR IT BUT IT'S SECOND-DEGREE
MURDER IN PLAIN AMERICAN,"
WAS THE WAY CASS PUT IT WHEN
LAN AND MAYEN TRIED TO PULL A
FAST ONE WITH A JADE WHOOZIS
THAT WAS HALF CAT, HALF
ELEPHANT.

CHAPTER ONE
CASS GETS A CLIENT

THE PHONE rings about ten thirty and the girl at the desk says: "Lieutenant MacAndrews calling!" and I say: "Send him up!" I might as well because if there was anything Mac wanted to see me about he'd come up anyway.

By and by he knocks and I open the door for him and another man and Mac looks at my pajamas and the bed not made up and says: "Pretty soft for some people—I got a half day's work done." Then he says: "This is Mr. Lan—" and to the guy with him: "This is John Cass, the man I was telling you about."

I shake hands and say: "Land?" and he says: "No. Lan. L...A...N" and pulls out a card and gives it to me. I take a look at him and figure he's cut it from Landous or Lanapoulas or some Greek name like that because there's Greek written all over him. He's short and dark and very smooth-looking—maybe forty.

Mac keeps looking at my pajamas with a disgusted look on his pan so I say: "I was trying to do something I know I can't do until about four this morning."

He says: "What?"

I say: "Trying to beat that creeper that Flynn's running."

Mac says: "Where was it last night?" and I say: "The Roslyn!" and to this Lan: "It's a traveling crap game."

Lan says: "I know!" so that's that. I can tell from looking at him that he's the kind that would know but I want to see if he'll admit it. I've always figured that a Greek kid's born with a pair of barbudi dice in his hands, they always got 'em in their pockets.

I ask them if they want a drink and they both say it's too early in the morning and then I sit down on the bed and they sit facing me and I look at the card he give me. It says—

HENRI LAN

365 Laurel Drive

Pasadena, California

IMPORTING   EXPORTING

It takes more than that Henri business to change him from a Greek to a Frenchman but it's none of my business what nationality he wants to pick. We all just sit there and stare at each other for a minute and when Lan sees I ain't going to ask him what they want he says to Mac: "Maybe you'd better tell Mr. Cass about—" and Mac puts his hand up and says: "You tell it."

Lan says: "Well, I was going to San Francisco today and the man who was to stay at my house while I was gone didn't come this morning as we had planned. I telephoned him and finally drove to his house here in the city to see what was wrong and he was—" He stops and looks at the floor and Mac finishes it with: "Dead!"

Lan says: "Yes, dead! I called the police at once and Lieutenant MacAndrews"—he waves at Mac—"came down and looked things over. I asked him who I could get to watch my house for me and he suggested yourself."

"You'll have to come
too, Mr. Cass."

I don't get the set-up. Why should anybody want to hire
a private dick for a watchman job? I say: "But why do you
need a detective, Mr. Lan?"

He says: "This man was murdered. I carry my stock in my
house, it's that kind of stock, and it is all very valuable. The
insurance companies won't carry me up to its full value."

Mac moves his chair so it's kind of back of Lan's and
says: "This guy was murdered and Lan thinks that it may
have something to do with somebody knocking over his
place. You get it?" Then he rolls his eyes at the back of
Lan's head and shakes his head first up and down and then
sideways. I get Lan's angle all right but what Mac is going
through all the motions for is by me.

I stall with: "I ain't doing nothing right now but I got
some stuff coming up. How long will you be gone?"

"Not more than a week," he says, "I have to go or"—he looks apologetic at Mac—"I wouldn't leave with this happening like this. My business in San Francisco cannot wait."

Mac still is making faces so I say: "It'll be a hundred for the week," and he says: "That's fine. When can you come? This has already delayed me more than I like." I can see Mac holding up one finger behind Lan's back so I say: "One o'clock."

Mac grins and Lan looks worried and says: "I should be on my way before then."

I say: "That's the best I can do. I'll have to see some people"—Mac nods his head on this—"and it will take until then to do it."

Lan says: "All right!" and counts out five twenties and then gets up and goes to the door and Mac follows him out but all the time motioning with his hand for me to stay in the room.

I get dressed and order breakfast brought up from the coffee shop and about the time I get through with it Mac knocks again and comes in and says: "I wanted to talk with you before you went out there."

I say: "I knew it was either that or a belly ache, the faces you were making."

He leans forward very confidential and says: "Johnny, this stiff had his throat cut damn near in two. But he didn't bleed hardly any."

I say: "Probably anaemic but let it go. I've just had breakfast."

He leans back sort of disappointed and says: "You don't get it. He wasn't killed there at his house, where Lan found him, but some place else and brought there."

I say: "Well, I didn't kill him so I wouldn't know."

He grunts and says: "Lan ain't coming clean with us, Johnny. This guy that was killed has worked for him about three years but we didn't find that out until we talked to the neighbors. Lan never said a word about it."

"What was this guy's name?"

"Nick Pappas. One Greek will always hire another Greek and that's what Lan is."

I say: "If Lan's clamming on you take him down and work on him." Mac just grunts. "You dope! This Lan is a big shot. He's got dough and friends and I ain't got either."

I tell him how he's breaking my heart but that after all he's the one that's working homicide for the city of Los Angeles and not me and that the thing's his business, not mine. He looks sad then and says how he's just telling me this so that I'll be watching out for myself, and I tell him that I'm always watching out for myself and that the reason he told me this is so I'll keep an eye out for him.

This is true and he grins and admits it but says just before he goes—"Just the same, Johnny, you watch your step. This dead man's about the nastiest-looking stiff I ever see and this Lan ain't telling all he knows." He goes out but sticks his head back in and says: "I forgot to tell you. Lan's got a cowboy all the time—he's taking him to Frisco with him. Ike Malloy. You know him?"

I do and plenty well. I had a beef with him once at a road house and he took a sucker shot at me and knocked me colder than a wedge and when I come to he was gone. I know him too well. I say: "Yes, I know Ike!"

Mac says: "Well, be seeing you."

THIS LAN'S got a swell place out in Pasadena right in the nice residential district, and I can't see how he can run an importing and exporting business in a house like that.

He meets me at the door and says: "I had better take you around and show you what is here and where it is. You'll have a better idea of where any attempt at breaking in will be made in case one is." He talks like he looks—very soft and smooth and easy and kind of purry. He hasn't got any accent at all. It sounds like he's learned words out of a book instead of by listening to people talk.

He shows me around then. Pretty near all the stuff in the house, outside of in the back where he lives, is what he calls "almost a museum piece." Stuff like jade and funny carved tables and chests and old vases and old rugs and things like that. A lot of it is put around to look as if it was being used but a lot of the smaller stuff is in glass cases against the walls, fixed so when they're opened a light shows on them. Even some of these rugs. He shows me a little one that he says is worth fourteen thousand.

He lives in the back of the place—very nice but nothing like the front where the people go, and while he's showing me this he tells me that he does a little general business with people that know him, old customers or people that old customers send to him, but that the most of his business is done on order. Somebody'll hire him to get something they've heard about in some other country and he'll get his agent there to get it for him and then make the deal.

He says that he's got at least two hundred thousand dollars worth of this stuff in the house and only blanket insurance for fifty of that.

The house is wired for alarms and he shows me all this but that don't mean a hell of a lot and I tell him so. A smart operator always has got that sort of thing lined out before he makes a move and there ain't an alarm system in the world that can't be beat if the guy knows what he's running into. Lan says he knows this and that's why I'm hired and then takes me and introduces me to the rest of the help.

Malloy I know already. He gives me a dirty look and don't offer to shake hands which shows he's half smart. We just say: "Hello," to each other and then Lan takes me to the kitchen and shows me the cook, who he says will watch the place in the day time when I'm sleeping. This cook is another Greek and has a name I wouldn't even try to get across.

He grunts at me and says something to Lan and Lan says to me: "He says for you to please keep out of the kitchen. He will call you when meals are ready."

I say: "That's O.K. by me!" and then I make a break. I say: "It's too bad that Nick Pappas got killed. I'd have liked to met *him*." I got no particular reason for saying it, just think that I want to see Lan's face. When I crack this I'm looking right at him and he don't blink an eye. He says: "That was a shame. Nick had been working here for three years almost, taking care of the grounds."

He's careful—too careful. Neither he or Mac had said anything about what the guy's name was when they was with me together and he *should* ask me how I know what the guy's name was and how I know he worked for him. He passes this though I know damn well he knows Mac must've come back and talked to me. I know I've made a break the minute I speak but it's too late then and I think that he probably knew Mac was wise all the time.

After he shows me how the alarm system is turned on and off—the control is right by the front door—and after he tells me he wants it left on all the time, he collects Malloy and they get in a big coupé and start out. He never says a word about why he's in such a hell of a rush to get to San Francisco and I can't very well ask him.

CHAPTER TWO
COOK'S TOUR

I LOAF around reading and looking at the different junk until about six when the cook comes in to where I'm at and says: "Dinner is ready."

He leads the way back to the kitchen and we eat together without saying anything more than, "Please pass the bread," or something like that. He talks as good English as Lan though, when he wants to, and he learned to cook plenty good wherever he did.

When I get through and start to leave I say: "Swell dinner!" and he kind of grins, which shows a Greek is human and likes a pat on the back same as other people.

I go back to the library and read until dark and then prowl through the house just to be sure everything's all right and about the time I get back to the library and settled down I hear a bell ring and go to the front door and peek out the little slide that's in the door. I see a bunch of law in uniforms and then I hear a noise behind me and look around and see the cook with a gun as big as they make. A Colt .45, just like I shoot; and the way he carries it he knows more than just how to cook.

He says: "Who is it?"

I say: "The law!"

He makes a face and says: "We'll act like we're not here."

"They've already seen me looking out and if I know my law they'll come in here with axes if we act like we're not here."

He says something in Greek that sounds like he doesn't like this and makes another face and turns and goes back to the kitchen and I turn off the alarm system and take the chain off the door and open it and a big red-faced mick that seems to be running the squad says: "You took your time." He's got stripes on his sleeves but he's in uniform like the rest of them.

I say: "Sorry, Sarge. There's an alarm system and I wasn't too sure how to cut it."

He looks down at what he's holding in his hand and says: "Then your name ain't Lan?"

I say: "Lan ain't here. I'm a private copper hired to watch this place and my name's Cass."

He looks down again and says just like he was reciting a piece: "This is a search warrant for the premises described as being located at Three Sixty-five Laurel Drive." He glances up at the number above the door to make sure he's at the right place and I try to stall him with: "I'm sorry. Mr. Lan ain't here. He'll be back in a week."

THE BIG mick stands there holding his warrant like he don't know what to do and just then a little short stocky guy in plainclothes, who I ain't noticed before, slides up next to him and says something under his breath to him and the big mick says: "It don't make any difference whether Lan is here or not. This is a search warrant and good whether he is or not." He waves his arm and the three coppers with him come ahead and he comes in with 'em, with me backing out of his way and with the little short guy tagging them.

I say: "Can I see the warrant?" and he hands it to me and I look it over and see it's what he says it is so I tell him: "Just go ahead. I hope to hell you're careful because a lot of this stuff might break and I'll be the goat if it does."

He grins and says that they'll be careful and for me to come along with 'em if I want, so I close the door and put the alarm back on and the six of us go through the place with me helping 'em all I can.

It's all I can do. I don't know what they're looking for or why they're looking for it but I figure it's better for me to keep an eye on what's going on. I know damn well that if I make a fuss about it I'll be taken down to the station and charged with resisting and that won't help things. This big cop's the kind of bird that ain't too smart but wants his way when he knows what it is.

At that, he's a hundred percent. He don't touch a thing and don't let any of the squad either, and after they've shaken the front of the place down I lead 'em back to where Lan and Malloy and the cook live and they go through that the same way. When they look through the kitchen the cook just sits on a table and don't say a word, which don't make me mad because I thought he'd raise hell with them and make jail and I'd have to cook for myself.

I notice finally that the cops seem to be looking around as if they don't know what they're looking for and don't expect to find it but that the little short guy is looking plenty close. I can't make him out, he don't act like he's a copper but I can't figure what he'd be doing there if he wasn't. By and by he drags behind to peek under something and I ask the big mick: "Who's the little guy with you, Sarge?"

He don't answer me for a while, but just pretends like he don't hear me so I do as good and pretend I ain't said a word.

The little guy is peeking under Malloy's bed and the mick and I are standing by the door and watching him and then the mick whispers: "It beats me. They just give me this warrant and told me to look the house over for anything that looks like stolen property. They just said that this fella was going along." He shakes himself and says: "A policeman does what he's told."

I could add something to this but I don't. I could tell him that Johnny Cass does everything a policeman tells him to do, that is, if the policeman's there to see that he does it and get tough if he don't. That's one thing about the law. They got the edge all the time and when that edge is helped by them having a search warrant I play on their side.

When they get through and start to leave the little short guy drags behind and says to me: "You ain't worked for Lan before, have you?"

I say: "Today's the first day I ever saw him."

He says: "You know Ike Malloy that works for him?"

I say: "Yes, the dirty rat! Too well." He kind of grins at this and says: "If I was you I'd watch my step with both of 'em."

I say: "Thanks! You're—"

He don't say a word but catches up with the mick and the rest of the squad and I turn off the alarm and let 'em out. The mick turns and says: "Thanks, fella. Be seeing you," and they go and I go back to the library and try and figure what it's all about and can't.

All I know is that Lan and Malloy are hot but what about I don't know and there don't seem to be any way to find out.

ABOUT AN hour after this the cook comes in and tells me he's going to bed and that I'm to hold the fort by myself and I tell him goodnight. Then I dig up a bottle of good rye that I've spotted and take a drink and read until eleven and then go through the house again and then back to the library and take another shot. I do the same thing at twelve and again at one and am sitting there reading about half past one when I hear a little noise and look up and see in the library door a guy standing there holding a gun on me. He says: "Stick 'em up!"

I do just that. If he was close I might have a chance to knock the gun away but the way he's got me that's no dice. I can't jump across fifteen feet of floor without getting shot on the way so I don't try any foolishness. I raise my hands without getting out of the chair and two guys come in from the hall past him and grab my arms and lift me out of the chair. Then they tie my hands behind my back with a piece of sash cord and then my feet the same way. Both these guys look like some kind of foreigners and the head man has got a face that couldn't be forgot. He's got a bum ear that hangs down in front like a dog's ear that droops and he's got a nose that's been broken a dozen times if it was once. And it looks like he never did bother to have it set.

When I'm tied this guy comes over and takes the gun out from under my arm and then he says: "You make no noise."

The house is set back from the street far enough that I could yowl at the top of my voice and never raise anybody so I say: "I won't!" and try and figure out just what breed of cat he is. He's got an accent that's a honey but one that's a new one on me. I know he's not wop or German or French but that's all.

They go out of the library and I hear 'em walk down the hall an' nothing more until in about half an hour I hear a siren on a police car and then I hear a bunch of feet running toward the back of the house and then I hear this alarm system turn loose and a big bell someplace on the roof starts clanging like hell. Then in a minute I hear a shot and then by and by somebody pounds on the front door.

I shout: "Break it down!" and then I hear an ax and pretty soon the same big mick that searched the joint earlier in the evening comes busting in with a gun in his hand. He sees me and says: "What's happened?" and I say: "Untie me."

He does and I start for the back of the house with him and two more guys in uniform right along with me. The cook's bedroom is on the second floor and looks out over the back yard and I head for there and go in and see the cook laying on the bed with his feet and hands tied. He's fixed up better than I was, too—he's got a towel wrapped around his puss and the towel holds another rag in his mouth so tight all he can do is gurgle. I yank this loose and we untie him and then he tells us that he went to sleep with his window open and that when he woke up a guy was standing by the bed with a gun on him. The guy tied him up and then let down a rope ladder through the window and two more guys came up and then they all went downstairs. I look out the window and see where a drainpipe from the roof comes right up alongside the window and I show this to the mick and we figure the first guy was enough of an acrobat to climb it.

We look through the house and can't find where anything is taken and then the mick tells me that some people going by in a car thought they saw somebody climbing in the window and telephoned the cops. He tells me they saw one guy running through the back yard and shot at him but missed and that the guy beat it in a car that was in the alley. I figure the other two had made the car first and were waiting for this last man.

He telephones the station and by and by a printman comes out and looks the place over and dusts a lot of powder on this, that and the other and takes a few impressions and pictures and the rest of the rigamarole they go through and then they all go home. It's about five o'clock by that time and daylight so I go to bed and leave the cook to finish and tell him to call me at twelve.

He don't. He calls me at eleven. I wake up and look past him and see MacAndrews and Mac says: "I hear there was doings last night."

I get up and get dressed and tell him all that happened and he says: "Did you wire Lan about it?"

I say: "Lan never said where he was going to be."

MAC LOOKS kind of sour and says: "That was really what I wanted to find out about. I wired Frisco and they were going to pick him up. I gave them what kind of a car he's got and the license number, but they missed him. I wanted him tagged while he was up there."

I say: "But not pinched!" and he says: "Hell, no. I ain't got anything on him. I just wish I had." Then he says: "The way this place is wired, how in hell did these guys get in and you not hear 'em?"

I say: "Cinch! This cook had the wires on his window hooked around so that he could open it without turning on the alarm. He figured because he was on the second floor he was safe."

Mac says: "You sure he wasn't in with these yeggs and let 'em in the back and let 'em tie him up so's it'd look good?"

I say: "When they heard the police car and ran out the back, everything worked. Every door is wired so that when it's opened it touches off a bell on the roof that sounds like a fire bell."

He looks disappointed and says: "This cook's a Greek and I never trusted a Greek." I ask him why and he says: "Like a damn fool I let one of them teach me to play barbudi once and I lived on coffee and doughnuts the rest of the month."

This barbudi is a Greek dice game and a honey if you don't all the time run out of money. I always do so I know how Mac feels. We go downstairs and I turn off the alarm and let him out and then turn it back on again and the cook goes out in the kitchen to get me some breakfast.

He's out there maybe five minutes and then I hear the bell on the roof go *CLANG—CLANG—CLANG.* By the time it's hit about three times I've got my gun clear and am out in the hall that leads back to the kitchen, and just then I hear a gun back there. I slam through the kitchen door and see the cook laying over the sill of the outside door and see it's wide open, and I jump over him and into the yard and see a guy running towards a car that's parked in the alley back of the house.

I shout at him: "Stop!" but the bell on the roof's making so much noise I never do know whether he hears me or not, but whether he does or not he doesn't stop running. I stand still so I'm good and steady and settle on him and just as he gets to the car I let go. He falls against the door but catches himself with his hands and a guy from inside the back leans out and tries to help him in the car and I aim for this one—what I can see of him over the one I've shot—and try it and shoot too low. I can see the guy I've already hit once jerk as the second slug hits him.

The guy that's trying to lift him in lets go and ducks back out of sight, and the car starts and the guy I've hit just slides off as it pulls away and goes down. I run out to the alley as fast as I can, figuring I may get a pop at the car, but just as I get to the alley it makes it around a bend so it's no dice.

I look at the mug that's laying there and see I took him center in the back with the first one and in the back of the head with the other. The bullet went on through and come out his face and I figure the guy that was hauling on him got ticked, but I don't figure hurt very bad because after a bullet goes through all the bone that's in a man's head it's lost so much force it can't do much harm. A .45 like I shoot has got a hell of a lot of shocking power but it isn't so good on penetration.

I run back to the kitchen and see the cook's managed to drag himself back inside but is still laying on his face so I turn him over and see that he's been shot in the belly. He's passed out so I leave him there and go in and shut off the alarm so the damn bell on the roof'll quit ringing and then call the law and tell 'em to bring an ambulance and a surgeon.

The clerk at the desk says:

"They're on their way already. I'll send the ambulance after them."

I hang up the phone and start to go back to the kitchen and see if I can do anything to help the cook, but before I get started I hear a siren coming so I stop and let the law in. It's the same big mick that's been here twice before and the little short guy's with him, the same one that looked the place over. They dash in and I lead the way to the back and show 'em the cook and the stiff out in the alley and about this time the ambulance and the surgeon comes and we load the cook on a stretcher and into the ambulance and they take him to the hospital, though the surgeon says he won't come to before he dies.

They load the stiff that's in the alley into the morgue wagon and about the time it pulls away with him I miss the little short guy and say to the mick: "Where's your friend?"

He says he don't know and we look for him and find him snooping through the house again and the mick says: "Le's go."

The little guy says all right and they start to leave and the mick tells me they'll print the dead man to try and find out who he is and that he'll phone what they find back to me. Just as they leave the little guy turns and says to me: "This is a bad place to get careless in!"

This leaves me something to think about while I'm waiting for the mick to call. In about an hour he does and says that there's no record in either Pasadena or Los Angeles of anybody with his print classification and that they're going to put his picture in the paper and hope somebody knows him and tells them about it.

That settles that night. I'm out a cook because Riley, that's the mick's name, calls about five that afternoon and says that he died about three hours after they got him to the hospital so I got to do my own cooking.

The next day Mac comes over again and says that the San Francisco police ain't picked up any trace of Lan and am I sure he went to San Francisco. I tell him that all I know is what Lan told me he was going to do and that's all I hear from Mac or anybody else.

CHAPTER THREE
THE CAT'S ELEPHANT

NOTHING HAPPENS for five days then and then Lan comes home. It's about six in the evening and I'm in the kitchen opening tin cans for dinner when I hear a car pull into the driveway and then the front door bell rings. I go to the door and peek out the little slide and see that it's Lan and that Malloy's with him and I let 'em in, after turning off the alarm. The first thing Lan says is: "I've been reading the papers. What a hell of a watchman you are."

I slide kind of to the side of the hall so that both he and Malloy are in front of me and can't gang up on me if there's fireworks and say: "You rat! Open that pan again to me like that and I'll knock your teeth out the back of your neck." Malloy starts to move ahead and toward me and I tell him: "You start something, baby, and I'll finish it."

Lan says: "No, no, Ike!" to Malloy, and to me: "I'm sorry, Cass! I guess I'm excited."

I say: "Wait until you find out what happened before you blow your cork then. I get excited too."

He says very nice: "I'm sorry. It's because I'm so worried." He heads past me for the library and Malloy follows him like a pet poodle but giving me the bad eye all the time. I go in there with 'em and Lan asks me to tell them just what happened and I do and then Lan says: "And you don't know who this little man is? The policeman wouldn't tell you!"

I say: "I don't think it was because he didn't want to tell me. I don't think he knew. He acted like he was told to take the little guy along and mind what the little guy said."

Lan and Malloy look worried and then Lan says: "Come on, Ike. Let's go and clean up before we eat."

I'm still sore about the crack he made in the hall so I say: "There's no more cook so it looks like you'll have to open your own canned stuff. I won't." I don't like him any too well anyway and I figure that I'll be damned if I cook for him.

He don't get mad or at least he don't show it but just says that he'll phone and have dinner sent in and then he and Malloy go to the back and upstairs where their rooms are and I sit down in the library and wait.

By and by Malloy comes back without Lan and sits across from me and stares at me and it takes me about five minutes to get sore enough to do something about it. I say: "Is there something you want?"

He says: "Nothing you can give me!" and then laughs very snotty and says: "I remember once at a road house I gave you something you didn't want."

I get the idea plenty now. I can't figure why he does, but he wants to start something—the way he's sitting in his chair and the way he's holding the bottom of his coat with his left hand so he can get at the gun under his arm is plenty tip-off. I'm sitting sort of on the small of my back and got both hands on the arms of my chair and with him ready like that I'm behind the eight ball so I stall for time.

I say: "Yes, you bet. And then took a powder before I come to—like the heel you are."

I straighten up a little in the chair and he comes out with the gun before I have a chance at mine and says: "This time you ain't going to come to." He don't cock the gun but just holds it on me. I figure that he thinks he can work the double action on it in plenty of time in case I make a play.

I say: "What in hell's the idea? You high or just crazy?"

He grins at me and says: "What d'ya mean, crazy?"

I say: "Crazy. MacAndrews, in the city, knows I'm here and Riley, one of the cops down here, knows it too. You must be crazy."

He laughs this nasty laugh again and says: "Sure! I'm going to load you in the car and dump you out on the highway. They may think something's phony but thinking and proving's two different things. They think I killed Nick Pappas too, but they can't prove it and you won't be able to help 'em on it."

I'M STILL stalling. This chair I'm in is pretty heavy and I've got a good grip on the arms of it and he's only sitting about five feet away. I say: "Didn't you?" and he says: "You know damn well I did. What the hell did MacAndrews plant you over here for? What was this little guy you're so proud of shaking the place down for? Knowing ain't proving. D'ya think I'm going to sit back and—"

He gets this far and I lift myself up by my hands on the chair so that my feet are aimed at his puss and kick out. I land on his face and neck and he goes back, with his chair on top of him and I land on my back on the rug, between his chair and mine. I get up just as he wins his wrestling match with his chair and gets up, and I manage to grab his arm with one hand and the gun with the other before he can shoot.

I got both hands busy trying to hold his right arm and this gun, and that leaves his left free and he starts smacking me in the face with it—hard, too. I get clear of him and see how he's standing and tramp down with my heel, aiming for his instep. I hit his shin first but there's still some power left when my foot slides down it to his instep and he howls like it hurts plenty and bends over until his head is about even with my waist and I bring my knee up in his face.

It'd knock any ordinary man out but this guy is an ex-pug. It just straightens him up. I put one leg back of his knee and shove him in the chest with my shoulder and he goes backwards, off balance, and when he does I let go of his arm and the gun and when he hits the floor I kick him in the face.

He can really take 'em. He's dazed some but he rolls away from me with me following him and trying to jump on him and put him out but I can't land solid the way he's whirling and all the time his head is clearing. Finally, after he's rolled half across the floor, he gets hold of my leg and yanks and I go down too. When I fall I manage to twist so's I can get hold of the gun and he don't expect this and lets go but it don't do me any good because I fumble it and drop it just as I get it.

We roll around on the floor there for another minute that seems like an hour and I'm getting all the worst of it. He's bigger than I am and he can hit about twice as hard and he's doing it. He's got a knack of putting his weight behind a punch, even when he's on the floor the way he is. I'm just having one hell of a time keeping him away from the gun but I manage it until he cracks me on the adam's apple with a good solid smack.

It don't put me quite out but there's time for him to get to his knees and get the gun and then haul himself up by holding onto a table and get to his feet. Then he starts aiming the gun at me and I start rolling away from him. He's in bad enough shape that it's hard for him to get me lined up and all the time I'm rolling I'm yanking my own gun out from under my coat and I finally end up against a davenport just as he shoots at me and misses.

I shoot back but just as the gun kicks in my hand I know I've shot high and hit him in the shoulder instead of low enough down to stop him. The slug whirls him partly around but he turns back and starts to lift his gun again and I take him again and then once more for good luck. I was lined on his belly the second time and he tipped ahead towards me as he fell and I figure the third one ought to have hit him in the head.

Maybe it didn't need that last one but a guy that tough is too tough to take chances with. He might still be able to shoot.

I manage to get to my feet and I'm so shaky it's a hell of a job. All I can do is manage to hold on to my gun and not drop it. I stagger over to him and turn him over and see I've called my shots—one high in the shoulder—one through the belly—and one right through the top of his head and ranging down through it. He's plenty dead. Then I get a hunch and turn around so's I can see the door and here's Lan standing in the doorway and holding a damn dinky little automatic about half-raised.

I don't know whether he'd have guts enough to shoot at me or not. Maybe with my back turned like that he might. I do know the minute he knows I see him he tries to hide the gun behind him.

I say: "Drop it on the floor."

He does.

"Get in here."

He does that, too.

Then I say: "There's the phone. Pick it up and say *'I want a policeman!'* "

I'd do it myself but I figure I'm too shaky to walk that far for a minute.

He looks at me and says: "Wait a minute, Cass!"

"Why?"

"Listen! We don't need the law on this."

Maybe he don't but I do. A self defense plea goes a lot better if the law is told about it right off the bat. The room and my face'd show self-defense but if I wait before I call, the law might figure I ain't leveling.

I keep looking at him and he says: "Now listen! Give me time to get out of here with a fair start and then call the law."

I say: "Get out of here where?" and he says: "For five thousand dollars you wouldn't care, would you? Cash!"

I'M STILL shaky but not so shaky I can't think. I stall him and ask: "But what of this shooting? There's liable to be law here whether they're called or not!"

He waves his hands and says that the room is so sound-proofed that nobody could hear the shooting. I ask him what the hell was the matter with Malloy, trying to pick a beef, and he hems and haws and says he don't know, which makes him out a liar.

Finally I say: "If I'm protected, maybe I wouldn't care where you go."

He says: "Oh I'm not going to stay away. It's just that I've got to get away now and that I'll be held as a material witness. I'm for you—not him." He waves at the body. "I'll back up any story you tell, if you'll give me a break now."

I say: "O.K.!" and tell him I want him to sign a statement that he saw the whole thing and that it was self-defense. He don't want to do it and puts up an argument and all the time I keep wondering what in the hell he wants to make a sneak for now, but can't make it add up. He finally says he will and sits down at his desk and writes it out and gives it to me and then says: "And now I can go, I'll be back in three or four days and I'll get in touch with you."

He gets up and starts for the door and I get up to tag along with him. I'm still trying to figure his angle. I know he got Malloy to try and knock me off and it's no part of my plan to let him go anyplace, though he don't know that.

When I made him come in the room he left the door into the hall about half open and just when he gets there I hear a clunking noise and he falls back and almost into me and then goes to the floor. He's only about six feet in front of me. I look up at the door, and see the same big guy that had broken into the house the first time—the same lop ear and the same broken nose. He says in the same funny accent to me: "Maybe he won't be back in three or four days."

He's got the gun he smacked Lan with pointed at my belly so I raise my hands without being told and a guy comes past this big man and takes my gun and stands over where he can watch me.

I say to this lop-eared monkey: "How in hell did you get in?" and he smiles very nice and says: "Through the back while you and this"—he reaches out and nudges Lan with his foot—"were arguing."

I wonder why the alarm never rang and remember I never turned the damn thing on after Lan and Malloy came home. I can't figure how the big lug knew this though, but in a minute he says: "I figured that I'd have time to do my business here while your alarm system was bringing the police and yet have time to be away but there was no necessity of that." Then he bows at me and says: "Thank you."

Lan's out colder than a wedge and the big guy looks him over and says something to the guy that's watching me that I don't understand but which I can see means for him to keep an eye on me and then reaches down and picks Lan up and dumps him on the davenport.

He goes out to the kitchen and brings back a wet dish towel and slaps him across the puss with it a couple of times and Lan opens his eyes and says: "Mayen!"

The big boy nods so hard his lop ear almost falls off and says: "Mayen! That's right. Then he bends over Lan and says: "Where is it?"

Lan says: "I'll not tell you!" and this Mayen grins like this was good news and starts to lift the gun he's holding.

Lan sings out: "I'll tell! I'll tell!" and Mayen looks sad and says: "I'd as soon make you."

He makes Lan get up and follows him out of the room and by and by when they come back Mayen's got about the funniest-looking whoozit I ever saw tucked under one arm. It's about a foot high and looks like half elephant and half cat. It's a kind of pretty bluish green and doesn't seem to be very heavy, though this Mayen's so big and husky he could have carried that big a chunk of lead and never showed it.

He says something to this guy that's watching me that I don't understand and then says to me: "I'm sorry, but I must protect myself. I'm going to have to take you along with Mr. Lan."

I say: "Take me where?" and he waves his hand that's got the gun in it and says: "You won't be hurt. The only thing is, don't make any noise."

I'm still trying to figure out his accent. He talks very plain but kind of as if he had to think of what word he wants to say. He's got the lightest eyes I ever saw in a man, almost white and looking like marbles. He's smiling but his eyes don't show it. The other guy says something to him and he growls something back and waves the gun at Lan and then at me so we go out the front door with him trailing us and into a sedan that's parked about half a block from the house. The other guy gets in the driver's seat and this Mayen gets in the seat with him after he puts us in the back and turns and leans over the seat so he can watch us and then we start.

CHAPTER FOUR
GREEK MEETS GREEK

WE GO through Los Angeles, keeping on San Pedro Boulevard, and then right on through. When we get past Compton this Mayen says to me: "I take you on a little trip on the ocean. You act all right and you'll be treated all right."

I say: "Why take me?"

"I can't take a chance on leaving you anyplace."

He shuts up and I think this over and can't see it makes sense. What he means is that he can't take a chance on knocking me off and having me found someplace. Whatever he's going to do to Lan I'd be a witness to and from the look in this bird's eye he knows a dead man can't go on a stand and testify.

We get to San Pedro and the driver eases down a street that leads to the docks and stops the car and gets out and this Mayen waves his gun at Lan and me and says: "Get out and keep quiet."

They make us walk out on one of these docks to where a launch is tied and make us get down in it and then we start out through the harbor. There's not a chance for me to make a break on the way and pretty soon it's too late. The guy that drove the car is running the boat and Mayen is watching us but he don't really have to watch me. I can swim but not very good and in about five minutes the launch is far enough out from shore that I know I couldn't make it back.

We go almost out the harbor and pull up beside a big boat and Mayen makes us climb a ladder and up to the deck and then makes us go downstairs into a cabin and puts the guy that's been with us all the time to watch us and then goes back on deck.

Just as soon as he goes Lan says something to this guy and the guy talks back to him and then Lan turns to me and says: "This man's a Greek. He can't talk English."

I say: "What's Mayen?" and Lan says: "He's half Russian and half Finlander. He's captain of this ship—it's a Greek boat though."

I say: "What's the idea of the snatch?"

"I guess he wants to hold me up for money. I've had some dealings with him and he knows I've got some. That's all I can think."

I say: "What was the whoozit he made you give him at the house?" and he tells me it's another of what he calls "museum pieces."

We sit there and wait and Lan fidgets around and talks a little Greek to this sailor and by and by the Greek comes out with a pair of barbudi dice and Lan says to me: "You play barbudi?"

I say: "I have!" and he says: "We might as well, to pass the time away."

When they searched us at the house all they did was take our guns away. I got about a hundred and thirty dollars and Lan's got close to five hundred and the sailor's got about twenty-five. Lan sizes this up and winks at me and takes the dice and puts out fifty on the table and the Greek puts his twenty-five on half of it and I take the rest and Lan pitches the dice and they show deuce trey which is no dice.

Barbudi's a Greek game but a good one. I always think a Greek can smell one because if one's started in a back room with the door locked, inside of fifteen minutes there'll be a dozen Greeks there and all with money in their hands just like they come out of the air. You win with a six-five or double ace, treys or fives and lose with an ace-deuce, fours or sixes and all the other points are no dice. To show how the Greek boys trust each other, the dice are very small and so rounded that you can't call a point with 'em like sometimes you can with a set of regular dice.

Lan makes a second pass and they show two fours and the dice go to the sailor because he's on the right. It goes left to right instead of right to left like a crap game. He takes 'em and leaves his fifty on the board and Lan takes forty of it and I take ten and the mugg rolls six-five and collects. I'm getting interested and so's Lan. Interested enough that when the boat starts just then I think what the hell difference does it make because I'm behind the eight ball just as bad one place as another.

WE GO on like that for about fifteen minutes with the sailor going like he can't miss. Every time he gets the dice he goes over for two or three passes and Lan never gets across. Every time Lan gets the dice I buck him but ease up on the sailor and because I just about break even when it's my dice I'm about sixty ahead when Lan's about broke. It's a fast game. The sailor gets the dice and throws a wad of money down and Lan takes fifty of it with the last fifty he's got and I only take ten of what's left.

The sailor looks at Lan and grins and says something in Greek to Lan and Lan says to me: "He says it's no good for you to try and make your money last because you aren't going to have any use for money any more. He says you might just as well let him win it off you as have it taken off you."

It's what I've figured but I hate to have it told me. I look at the sailor and he grins at me like he was sorry and shakes his head too bad and just then the boat stops. With the engine quiet like that we can hear a lot of shouting on deck but it's all foreign so I don't know what it means but the sailor does all right because he drags out the gun he's shoved into his waistband and starts over to the door that opens on the steps we come down, in a hell of a hurry.

He gets his back to me when he does this and I dive at him and get him right at the knees. He drops the gun and falls back sort of on top of me but he's a little guy and I don't have any trouble in twisting around and socking him on the jaw. I do this and he goes out and about the same time Lan reaches for the gun that's skidded across the floor. He ain't in any hurry and I jump and beat him to it and jab him in the belly with it and say: "Back up."

I take a look around and find some rope underneath some built-in seats along the wall and tell him to face the wall and tie his hands behind his back. He meauws like hell about this and says: "Why tie me up?"

I say: "It looks like it's going to be every man for himself and you'll be just one less to watch."

I lay him on one of these seats and tie his feet and then get the sailor, who's still out, and lay him on another of these seats and tie him up the same way.

The shouting is still going on up above so I take off my shoes and see the gun I took off the sailor is full of shells and open the door that goes upstairs real easy and sneak up them so I can take a look.

I see plenty. There's enough noise going on so's I could have left my shoes on and done a tap dance and nobody would hear it. Everybody that I can see is lined up along one side of the boat and staring over and everybody's talking at once. I see Mayen standing there right close to me—it's about fifteen feet to the side of the boat, and I sneak up a ways to where a clear place is on the side with a boat hanging there that I can hide behind so he can't see me, and look over to see what all the excitement's about.

There's another boat, maybe a hundred yards from us, and it looks about half as big as ours. We look like we're maybe four or five miles from San Pedro and this other boat is between us and the town so that it's outlined plain. Between us and this other craft is a rowboat coming our way and it looked like there's about a dozen men in it. Just as I see this there's a shot comes from the front of our boat and Mayen shouts something and busts away from this rail and comes tearing back past me and goes in a house affair that's on the deck and right level with where I'm standing. He don't see me at all.

I go over to the side of this deck house and look in and see him pulling a rifle off hooks on the wall so I go to the side of the door and when he comes out I clout him on the head with my gun and hit plenty hard. He goes down and I know he's going to stay down for some time. I grab the rifle and look and see it's loaded and then stand back so all these guys along the rail are outlined and then I shout: "Everybody stick 'em up."

Some of them turn and some don't. I see a guy about fifty feet down with a gun in his hand and when he comes up with it I try one at him and he goes down and the minute I shoot all those that ain't turned turn plenty quick.

I shout at them again and swing the gun back and forth and they keep turned and watch me instead of the rowboat. By and by these guys in the boat hail us and I say: "A couple of you birds let down that ladder so's the company can come up!" And there must be some of them understand English because two of them do this.

THE FIRST guy up is the little short guy that was at Pasadena looking through the house, then comes a guy in uniform and then a bunch of sailors. Seven or eight of these. The guy in the uniform sees what the score is and has the sailors watch these guys I've been watching and then he and the little short guy come over to me and I put the rifle down and let them take over.

The uniformed guy says: "Did you shoot at our boat?" He's got a gun in his hand and it's pointed at me.

I say: "Hell, no! I shot at that guy that's laying on the deck over there."

He goes over and looks at this bird I've shot and the little guy says to me: "Where's Lan?"

I say: "Now wait a minute. Who're you?"

He says: "Arthur Josephs." He pulls out a gold badge that I see is federal and I say: "I got Lan on ice downstairs."

He tells me to wait a minute and goes down the line of men that the sailors are watching and comes back with the uniformed man and says: "I guess we missed him. He must have got away."

I say: "Who got away?" and he says: "Karl Mayen. The captain."

When I smacked Mayen he fell in the shadow of this little house and he's hard to see. I say: "There he is!" and point him out and the little guy gurgles like he's found his sweetie and reaches down and puts cuffs on him.

Then we take him downstairs to where Lan is and the first thing Lan says when he sees the uniformed man is: "Let me loose! I've been kidnaped."

It's a good bluff but it don't get over. The uniformed man looks at Josephs and Josephs says: "All in good time." He looks at me and says: "What do you want him for? Tied up like this."

I say: "I'm taking him back to Los Angeles to turn him over to the homicide department. He hired a heel named Malloy to kill a guy named Nick Pappas and then he hired him to kill me because he thought I knew something about it. This last kicked back on Malloy." Then I say to Lan: "The Greeks have probably got a word for it but in American it's second-degree murder."

The little federal man grins at him and says: "There's other words too. Such as possession of stolen property and conspiracy to evade payment of duty on imports and false entry on citizenship papers and false income-tax reports and a lot of words like that." He waves at Mayen then and says: "He's in on a lot of things like that, too."

He sees the little half elephant and half cat thing that Mayen brought from Pasadena with him and says: "That will get them plenty right there. That cinches 'em."

I say: "What in hell makes that so important?"

He laughs and tells me that the thing was made out of jade, in China, long before any of the Chinese jade workers ever saw an elephant. Somebody from some other country told them what an elephant looked like and they tried to make a model of one but they weren't sure of their dope and put cat in the doubtful places. It seems the thing was stolen from a San Francisco collector and that Josephs knew Lan had a sale for it and figured sooner or later it'd turn up at

Lan's house. This is what he kept looking for and now that he's got it, it makes Lan a fence and Mayen a thief.

On the way back from Pedro I learn all I didn't know before. Lan and Mayen have been working together—Mayen bringing stuff in from foreign places and Lan selling it for him. They didn't pay duty on this stuff at all and this little Josephs has been watching them for some time trying to hang it on them. Mayen swipes, or has somebody swipe this elephant doo-hickey and Lan don't pay him off for it so Mayen tries to steal it back while Lan's out of town trying to sell the thing to somebody. The first time he tries it he gets scared away, and the second time one of the guys with him gets panicky and kills the cook. The little federal man starts watching the house after this and sees Lan and Malloy come home and then sees Mayen and another guy come in and take Lan and me and the elephant thing out and he follows us and gets a coast guard boat to help him make the pinch.

He don't know but he thinks Lan had the elephant in a handbag with him while he was gone, I suppose because he couldn't find it in the house.

He's got a case against Lan and Mayen without this thing at all but he ain't taking any chances on not making it stick.

About this time we get in to Pedro and take Lan to Los Angeles and turn him over to MacAndrews and the next day I go up with him and get cleared on killing Malloy. It's a cinch—Lan's statement would do it alone without putting in anything about them being afraid of me on the Pappas business, and wanting me out of the way on that to help.

I don't see Mac then for about a week and then he says: "Both Lan and Mayen figured they couldn't beat any of that federal stuff or stolen property and took the rap on all of it. Homicide slid out on it—we knew damn well we couldn't stick Lan for having Malloy try and kill you and, with Malloy dead, the Pappas killing wouldn't hold any better. We know he hired Malloy to do it but knowing and proving is two different things. Mayen'll get at least ten and Lan twenty and up and they'll both get deported afterwards so what the hell."

I say: "What made Lan have Malloy knock Pappas off, d'ya suppose?" and he grunts and says: "We won't ever know. Pappas probably crooked him some way and he found it out—none of them guys ever leveled in their life."

I ask about the guy I shot on the boat and Mac tells me he was only shot through the ham and not hurt much and is getting along O.K.

There's been something bothering me every time I think of it and I figure maybe Mac might know the answer. I say: "How come Lan ever hired Malloy to cowboy for him? You'd think Lan would have hired a Greek—one Greek always hires another Greek."

He says: "Not always. Lan hired you." Then he laughs and says: "Malloy's name was Makalous, you dope. The closest he ever came to Ireland, in spite of that name Malloy, was when his boat came across the ocean from Greece."

CURTAINS FOR FIVE

WHEN BLEYER AND OLSON TOOK THE CASE IT LOOKED LIKE A SIMPLE DIVORCE FOR ONE, INSTEAD OF CURTAINS FOR FIVE

B **LEYER SAID:** "Just a minute, Mrs. Kargen!" to the woman across the desk from him, then called: "Miss Jorgenson!" through the open door to the outer office. When a blond girl came to the door he asked: "You raise him?"

The blond girl said: "He's on his way."

Bleyer said: "Fine!" and after the blond girl had stared at the woman at the desk for a moment, went out, he said: "He'll be here right away."

The woman shrugged trim, tailored shoulders, said: "I'll wait then." Her voice suggested she wasn't used to waiting. She looked at Bleyer for a moment, opened a brown cloth handbag that matched her jacket, reached inside it without taking her eyes from Bleyer's and took out a man's flat billfold. She reached inside this, still without looking away, and took out three yellow bills. She held them across the desk, said: "For a retainer."

Bleyer waved them back, said: "We're not retained yet!" in a short voice. His dark face looked angry and he drummed on the desk with his fingertips as he added: "I've got a partner to consider or I'd tell you now that we won't be."

The woman shrugged again, looked down at the desk and spread the money out across in front of her. She said: "I didn't know private detectives were so—careful."

She accented "careful" and Bleyer said impatiently: "Now I've explained that. We'll go for some things and leave some things alone and this looks like one we leave alone. We've just started in and we got a license to lose and a fee ain't worth taking a chance on." He looked at the money, saw the small *100s* in the corners of the bills, added: "But we'll see what Mr. Olson thinks," a little hastily. He looked up as he heard a door in the outer office slam, said: "Here he is now," and to the man that came in, "Oley, this is Mrs. Kargen. Mrs. Kargen, this is Mr. Olson, my partner."

OLSON WAS short, blond, almost pudgy, wore a constant smile that fitted his china-blue eyes. He said: "Meetcha!" with a bow, saw the money on the desk and opened his eyes wide. He sat down at the end of the desk, said: "Ingrid said you wanted me in a hurry!" and looked again at the three bills that fronted Mrs. Kargen.

Bleyer said: "Maybe, Mrs. Kargen, it would be better if you told this to Mr. Olson. We had decided not to accept divorce cases but it depends entirely upon what Mr. Olson decides about it." He looked at the money in turn.

The woman turned to Olson, smiled confidently, said: "It's really simple. I'm married."

She paused a moment and Olson said: "Yes'm!"

"My husband, for this past year, has been away from home a good many times without any explanation. I think he's—" She hesitated again.

Olson, still looking at the money, supplied: "Cutting corners!" in a helpful voice.

"Yes, that's it. Exactly."

"Hell! I tried to give him a break," Olson said.

"And you want us to find out and prove it to you?"

"Yes."

"Prove it to you or to a court?"

She hesitated and Bleyer broke in with: "I told Mrs. Kargen, Oley, about our rule for divorce cases. I explained to her what we'd do and what we wouldn't."

The woman said: "Understand, Mr. Olson, it isn't a question of having to manufacture evidence. If I wasn't sure in my own mind I wouldn't ask for proof. I've got to have proof."

Olson asked: "But Mrs. Kargen! Why be so insistent on us taking this?"

"My husband has a violent temper and I'm afraid that when he finds out I'm having him followed… I'm afraid of him. He's—well, I'd rather have someone I can depend on, is all."

"You mean he's liable to get tough?"

"He's liable to do anything. This last year he's not been himself. He even carries a gun all the time."

"Why don't you get out?"

She said: "I'm afraid to." Olson looked at her and she hesitated, shrugged sharply and said: "I might as well show you so you'll believe me," in a resigned voice. She stood up, took the brown jacket off and showed both arms covered with greenish-black bruises. She redonned the jacket, said: "My back is worse," very simply. "I told him I was going to leave him and he—objected. He swore to me there is no other woman, but there must be."

Olson looked from her to the money on the desk, said to Bleyer: "Well, we might as well take it." Then he asked: "Where do you live?" and when she told him: "Nine Twenty-six El Cerrito Avenue," he made a note of it on a desk pad.

She said: "I didn't tell you before, but he's an amateur aviator. He goes in his plane to meet this girl so she must live out of town." Her voice was suddenly vicious.

Olson looked up sharply, asked: "What was the secret about that?"

She caught herself, answered him with, "I thought that might make it harder to follow him and that it might influence you not to take the case."

Olson grunted, asked: "Where's he keep the plane?"

"Glendale Airport. I followed him once but he went away in the plane and I couldn't follow that." She stood up and Bleyer went to the door with her.

"Shall we mail you the reports?" he asked.

"It would be better if I stopped here after them."

Bleyer said: "You're probably right. Wait about a week." He watched her go down the corridor with an ugly dissatisfied look on his face, swung back into the office and saw Olson showing the blond girl the three hundred-dollar bills and said: "Damn it, Swedes! This is dynamite."

OLSON SAID: "The money's good and we need it." He waved one of the bills in the air, said: "Rent!" waved another, said: "Groceries!" waved the last and said: "And liquor!"

Bleyer reached out and took the last, said: "No liquor. Won't you ever learn?" and to the girl, "Wha'd you think of her, Ingie?"

Ingie said: "In the first place I'm a Dane not a Swede!" and thoughtfully, "She's about thirty-three—maybe thirty-five. She's harder than nails. She used to be a swell-looking gal and can still get by. She's got at least five hundred dollars' worth of clothes on her back so she's got money. That's all."

Bleyer said: "No, it ain't! You should put in that she's lying by the clock, but I don't know where. If she's so damn scared of her old man, she'd get the hell out where he couldn't find her instead of getting evidence for a divorce. For that matter, she could get it on cruelty right now. Her whole story's screwy."

Ingrid Jorgenson said: "It's you that's screwy!" in a scornful voice. "All's the matter with her is that she's nerts over her papa and she's hoping to find out he's chiseling and praying to God she won't. She's so jealous she's about half crazy."

Olson said: "Why'd she pick us?" and Bleyer handed him a printed card that read, *Los Angeles Police Department,* and in the corner, *Lieutenant-Detective Paul Kowalski*. The card was scrawled across in ink with Kowalski's signature and Olson said: "That's a good Pole. Always gives a pal a break! Did I ever tell you about the time me and him went to pinch—"

Bleyer said: "You have! Suppose you give your old pal a ring and see what he knows about this. I got a hunch."

He listened to Olson talk to Kowalski, said irritably when this was over: "Then all he knows about her is that he found a stolen car for her once, and that when she asked him to recommend someone he picked us. He don't know anything about her. I'm scared of this and I don't know why."

"We still need the money. This may be all right."

"Yes, it may."

The blond girl said: "Just a big scaredey cat, eh?"

Bleyer looked over, saw her sitting on the desk and swinging her feet. He said impatiently: "Who asked you in this, Ingrid?"

The blond girl smiled, showing very even white teeth, said: "Miss Jorgenson to you, mugg! Does pay day come out of the three hundred? I missed last month and I eat, too."

Bleyer grinned back reluctantly, wadded up and tossed her the bill he had taken from Olson and said: "You get Oley's whisky money, Miss Jorgenson!"

She caught it, said: "And a very good thing, too." She smiled nicely again, said: "I'll take you both to lunch!" and started to put the bill in her purse.

Bleyer grunted to Olson: "Damn this weakness of mine for Swedes." He looked at the girl, added: "But what a pretty Swede!"

The girl looked up, said: "Dane, honey, and you know it."

Bleyer grinned at Olson, spread his hands, told her: "Well—Dane, then."

LEAVING OLSON to watch Kargen's house, Bleyer made inquiries at the Glendale Airport. He learned that Kargen's ship was a low-winged monoplane, heavily powered and painted a dark gray, almost a black. Casual questioning told him Kargen was tall and dark and heavy and possessed of a notorious temper.

The attendant he was talking to volunteered: "Mr. Kargen, he takes that ship out all hours of the day and night, and the Lord knows where he goes. He never says." Bleyer made his eyes blank and vacant and the man went on with, "And always by himself. He acts like he's got to get someplace right then and there."

Bleyer looked sly, offered: "Maybe he's got some gal on the string in some other town." He nudged the attendant in the ribs with his elbow. "Maybe he's married and can only get away at odd times."

The attendant said: "Well, maybe!" in a doubtful voice and Bleyer turned the conversation away from Kargen.

Bleyer hung around the main part of the afternoon, succeeding in buying the man several glasses of beer during the course of it, and was on hand with him in the status of an old and valued friend when a heavy coupé drove up.

The attendant said: "Here's Kargen now."

Bleyer saw the battered roadster he and Olson jointly owned stop a half block down the parking space, and wandered over to Kargen's plane with the attendant as it was run out of the hangar. He heard Kargen's curt, "Is it filled up?" and the answering, "Yes sir!" Then casually he moved away and met Olson by the car and told him: "We can't do anything here because they don't know where he goes. I've figured how to find out, though." He drew a list of towns from his pocket, with the plane's license number, said: "You can get Kowalski to make a few asks for you, can't you? He can find out if the plane lands in any of these where we can't."

Olson agreed this was likely and they drove back to the Central Station, found Kowalski, and after overruling a few objections persuaded him to send inquiries to all the landing fields within a radius of two hundred miles. With Kowalski's promise to call them as soon as he had any information they drove back to their office.

Ingrid Jorgenson met them as they came in, said: "Well, thank the Lord! All afternoon I've been trying to find you. Mrs. Kargen called and wants either one of you—the first one to come in—to call her. She's called four times."

Bleyer grunted: "Get her, hunh?" and when the girl got the number, said: "Mrs. Kargen! This is Otto Bleyer." He listened a moment, said: "But why did…" listened a moment more and slammed the phone down. He turned to Olson, said: "This gets me," in a puzzled voice. "She says drop the whole thing."

Olson said: "Drop the whole thing!" and gloomily, "The first case and the first dough we get our hands on in a month and more."

"She says keep the dough."

"Then we win." Olson brightened.

Bleyer's dark face was mystified. "And after her being so hot for us to take it. Did she say anything to you, Ing, about why she changed her mind?"

The blonde said: "She did not. I told you she was half crazy and jealous. Her old man probably called her 'honey' by mistake so she changed her mind."

Bleyer said: "Well, we make the difference between the three hundred and the wires we sent so we should fret. She probably told him she hired us and he talked her, or scared her, out of it."

Olson grunted: "Well, that's that. Let's the three of us go in the inside office and play some pinochle while we wait for another customer with three hundred bucks. Ingie's got some dough to play for now and we might as well get it."

WHEN TWO hours later the door to the anteroom slammed, Ingrid had just melded a run of trumps and a hundred aces. She said: "And a club marriage makes two-seventy. Somebody would come in when I've got the best hand I've had yet!"

She went to the outer room, closing the door after her, and Olson said: "If this hand's the best yet, it's a pip. I'm four and a half in now," in a sorrowful voice.

Bleyer held up his hand for silence and they heard heavy feet tramp through the outer room, saw the door open and frame a man. The blond girl was hanging to his arm and they heard her say: "But maybe they don't want to see you!"

Olson laughed and said: "It's all right, Ingie! This is Paul Kowalski."

Ingrid gave Kowalski's arm a jerk, snapped: "Is that any reason he can walk past me like that?"

Kowalski ignored her, blurted out: "I told you! I told you guys I didn't want in on that wire deal."

Both Bleyer and Olson stared at him and Ingrid dropped his arm as he went on with, "I'll go before the board for this."

Bleyer asked: "What's happened?"

Kowalski sat on the desk, mopped his forehead with his sleeve and said: "Plenty. And then some. A guy delivering groceries reported a stiff in the alley back of the nine-hundred block on El Cerrito and the homicide boys go out and find it's Kargen's chauffeur. That's all. They'll be looking for Kargen and find out I sent those wires and that'll fix me up."

Bleyer asked: "How?"

Kowalski snapped: "I'm not supposed to be digging up stuff for you guys. I signed those wires as if I was on a case. I get private information on the strength of my badge and pass it on to you."

Bleyer argued: "But you didn't get us anything yet!"

"What difference does that make? I signed the wires."

"I guess that's right."

"Sure, it's right. All you ever did is work for agencies. Ain't I right, Oley?"

Olson said: "You are. Anybody know about the wires yet?"

"No. They'll find out as soon as they begin to check up on Kargen."

"Have they talked to Mrs. Kargen yet?"

"They're all up there."

"You get us in and we'll get Mrs. Kargen to back up a yarn that'll clear you. If she claims she was sick and just had to get hold of her old man and asked you to do it for her you'll get over. Your story is that you knew you shouldn't do it but you was sorry for her and couldn't see any harm. It'll only mean a reprimand."

Bleyer looked bewildered, asked: "But what difference does it make whether he did it for her or for us?" Olson snapped: "Just our license. That's all. It's a damn sight different doing a favor for someone with an address on El Cerrito than it is helping out two private detectives on their first case. They'll take our ticket if they catch us off side and they'll suspend Kowalski for playing on our team." He grabbed Kowalski by the shoulder, said: "Come on! I know what I'm doing!" and started for the door. He said to the girl: "If anybody calls, tell 'em we'll be back pretty soon."

"O.K. What about my four and a half?"

"Damn your four and a half." And to Bleyer, "Come on, Otto."

"Shall I tell 'em where you're gone?"

"Tell 'em you don't know."

The blond girl watched them go through the door, turned and stared at Bleyer's desk, still littered with the pinochle deck. She stuck out her lower lip, said: "I know where you can go and your four and a half with you." She went to the desk, picked up her discarded hand, said: "I'll never get another one like that!" in a mournful voice.

NINE TWENTY-SIX El Cerrito Avenue had three police cars, one morgue wagon, and at least fifty other parked cars in the street before it. The drivers of these last, attracted by the sight of police cars and the possibility of witnessing a raid, had practically blocked the street in front of the house and Olson, swinging the roadster close to the clustered cars was waved back by a uniformed man who was trying to clear the tangle. Olson grunted to Kowalski: "Do your stuff!" and the uniformed man, seeing Kowalski's badge, grudgingly allowed them to park.

Kowalski got out, asked: "Who's on it?" and the policeman growled: "Casey and Loward!" Kowalski said: "Thanks!" and Olson explained to Bleyer: "If you don't know it, one's a good Joe and the other's a heel. I know Loward too damn well. Did I ever tell you about when me and Shorty Collins was on—"

Bleyer said: "You have! We going to have trouble getting to talk to Mrs. Kargen?"

"Dunno. If only Loward wasn't...."

They came to the door of the house and Kowalski took them past the guard on the door and just inside they met a tall, very thin, man.

Olson said: "Hi, Loward!" and the thin man smiled unpleasantly, asked: "And what's a private shamus doing on a homicide case? Riddle me that."

Olson said: "We got a client here. Any harm in seeing a client?"

Loward saw Kowalski behind Olson and lost the smile. He said: "And have you got a client here too? Or are you just along for the ride?" He said to Olson: "Out and stay out!" and to Kowalski: "If you're still on car recovery you don't belong here. Play around me and you'll hear me meauw later on, where it'll do some good." He turned and said to another man who came into the hall: "We got company, Pat."

Casey was as tall as Loward but at least twice as heavy. His nose had been broken and set crookedly and this gave his face a pleasant leer when he smiled. He smiled now, said: "What the hell, Lowey! What skin off your neck is it if Kowalski wants to come and see real detectives work. He wants to learn something." He grinned at Kowalski, shook hands with Olson and, when Olson introduced Bleyer, said: "Glad to know Oley's partner. I've known Oley a long time. You know he rated second man on the pistol team and they brought us plenty of medals."

Bleyer said: "Yeah, I've heard that. Several times."

Casey laughed and patted Olson on the shoulder and said: "Just an artist with a gun!"

Loward growled: "He may be an artist but is that any reason we should let him talk to Mrs. Kargen?"

Casey turned on him, asked: "Why not? What's the harm?"

Loward muttered something and went out the door and Casey said: "Poor Lowey! He hates Olson's guts and he hates private agencies and he don't think a hell of a lot of me."

Olson said: "Listen Pat! Is Mrs. Kargen in on this?" in a serious voice.

Casey reached up and fumbled his nose, looked sidewise, asked: "Is she? You'd know more'n we do." He gave his nose a vicious yank and admitted: "Until we find out something to go on, we don't know who's in it. Her old man may be able to tell us something and we're going—" He saw the slight grin on Olson's face and stopped.

Olson said: "We looked for him a while ourselves, if that's what you mean." He turned, saw that Loward was out the door, said softly: "If you'll keep that heel of a Loward out of it and see that you and Kowalski split the credit I'll give you a tip."

"Go on."

"Stake out the Glendale Airport. That's your only chance. Get it?"

Casey leered and said: "Thanks, Oley! I'll remember this."

He followed Loward out the door and Olson told Bleyer: "He hates Loward's guts but he's got to work with him. He's boss of the pair else we wouldn't be here." He saw a maid down the hall, called: "Hey, sister!" and when the maid stopped, told her: "We want to see Mrs. Kargen."

The maid looked doubtful and said: "I don't know," and Olson nudged Kowalski.

Kowalski pulled his badge from his pocket, said: "I'm sorry but it's important."

They followed the girl to a library, waited a few moments and when Mrs. Kargen came in explained the purpose of the visit.

She said: "Why surely. I'll tell the same story you gentlemen tell." Olson, at her side, Caught the jerk of her head and leaving Bleyer and Kowalski followed her to the other side of the room. She said: "I didn't want Mr. Kowalski to hear this. Can I see you tomorrow? At your office?"

"We'll be there, one of us, all day. Why not have Kowalski hear it?"

She hesitated for a moment, said: "Just a notion. Will anyone stop me?"

"Why should they?"

"Well—with the chauffeur being killed."

"We told the man in charge you were our client. You might be followed but it won't mean anything."

She said: "Some time tomorrow then!"

They drove the relieved Kowalski back to the Central Station and went back to their now closed office. Bleyer unlocked the door and when they went in Olson saw a note lying on the typewriter, said: "I guess somebody must've called." He picked up the note, read it and grinned: "Our Ingie's mad!"

He read aloud: "Oley. It's still four and a half you owe me in spite of the rush act. You'd make *me* pay."

Bleyer said: "You'd think she was a Yid instead of a Swede!"

Olson corrected him, said: "Dane, Otto. She says so herself."

MRS. KARGEN came in the office at twelve the next day. She hurried in, glancing behind her, pulled back a heavy veil, and Olson said: "If anybody's following you that ain't going to help a bit. Did your husband get back?"

He motioned to a chair and she sat down, said: "No. I knew he wouldn't. That's why I wanted to see you—that is, about him." She looked around the office questioningly.

Olson said: "They've gone to lunch on my four and a half," in a sour voice.

She looked blank and he said hastily: "Office politics! Just what is it?"

"It's about my husband again."

"Why all the hush stuff about coming up here?"

"I don't want anybody to know you're working for me."

"I didn't know we were. You called that off."

She said: "I know the police think my husband killed the chauffeur. Don't they?" Olson shrugged, didn't answer for a moment, and she insisted: "Don't they?"

He said: "Very likely they do now. I don't know as I'd blame 'em. The plane he went away in hasn't landed at any field within four hundred miles of here, as near as can be found out."

"Are you sure of that?"

"Kowalski just called me. They figure he landed on the Mexican side of the border but there's not much chance of finding out where."

The woman watched Olson's face as she said: "But he couldn't have killed Jerry. I saw Jerry after he left."

"Jerry?"

"The chauffeur." She caught Olson's smile, said: "I really did." Her eyes were anxious, worried.

Olson said: "I don't doubt it but if it comes to a trial a jury will." He asked: "Who do you think did do it?" and believed her when she said: "I don't know. I didn't sleep last night trying to think who would have."

"What do you want of us?"

"I want you to find out who did it."

"Why? You're in the clear. This beats divorcing your husband. It's less trouble for you."

She looked down at her hands, twisted a handkerchief between them, said: "I know that," very low. "I've changed my mind about that. I don't want to divorce"—she started to cry—"him."

Olson turned his light blue eyes to the ceiling, whistled softly, said: "Well, you ain't divorced him yet so why cry about it. What made you think he wouldn't be home last night?"

"He never comes home the same night he goes away like that."

"If he's heard about this, he won't be home for some time. Even if he is innocent."

"I know he's innocent."

Olson stared at her, said: "What if he ain't? If he did it and we find it out, it ain't going to make any difference whether we're working for you or not. You realize you're taking a chance when you start this, don't you?"

"I'm not. You forget I saw Jerry after he left. I know that."

Olson shrugged, said: "It's going to cost dough. People that kill other people in alleys are bad people to play around with."

"I've got money. How much will it be?"

"That depends on how long it takes. If there's trouble"—he shrugged again, watched her face—"it'll be plenty."

"You've got to find out. No matter what it costs."

They heard the door in the outer office open and Ingrid called: "Your four and a half went—" Then they saw her in the open door. She said: "Oh excuse me," went to one side and they heard her whisper to Bleyer.

He came in, stood just inside the door, said: "Hello, Mrs. Kargen—" and they heard Ingrid scream, shortly, harshly. At the sound Bleyer swung. As he faced the outer office they saw an arm shove him in the chest as he was off balance. He stumbled backward and Olson came to his feet and jerked at the gun under his arm, and at the same time another man took Bleyer's place in the door, a man who held a short black automatic in his left hand. The man moved the muzzle of the gun, said: *"Unh!"* and Olson jerked his hands up. The man said: "O.K., Joe! Come on in!" and stepped clear of the door.

Ingrid backed in followed by another man who held his hand in his side coat pocket. Ingrid turned her head, said to Olson: "We never saw them come in. They must have followed us in the door—"

THE MAN with his hand in his pocket had a smooth, very pale face. His eyes seemed everywhere in the room, flashing from Olson to Bleyer to Mrs. Kargen, and to Ingrid. He said: "Shut up, tart!" in a very soft voice and she glanced at Olson and Olson nodded his head. The man said: "Over against the wall!" in the same smooth voice, moved his coat pocket in the direction of the wall across from the desk and Olson and she backed over there. She stood straight against it with her hands at her sides. Her hands were clenched so the knuckles showed white, she looked more angry than afraid.

Mrs. Kargen stood up. She wore a surprised look, said to Olson: "Why, what is—"

The pale man said: "You too!" and she stopped, stood still and looked at him. He took a step forward and slapped her across the face with his right hand, the blow sounding loud in the quiet room. He said: "Jump!" But he didn't raise his voice; it still held the same soft tone.

She moved to the wall beside Ingrid, felt of her cheek, said: "Well..." in a startled, still unfrightened way.

Ingrid said: "Ain't this a bang!"

The man said to Olson: "You too!" and to Bleyer: "Line up!"

Olson saw the man at the side of the door swing the automatic his way, saw the pale man's eyes tighten. He said: "Yes you bet!" and moved to the wall and stood by Mrs. Kargen, and at the same time Bleyer lined up alongside of Ingrid.

The pale man said: "Very pretty picture!" stood in front of them with his head on one side studying them.

Olson said: "What's the idea?"

The pale man said: "Shut up and listen!" He moved his coat pocket toward Mrs. Kargen, said: "She's poor pipples to play with. Get it!"

Olson snapped: "And why?"

The man said: "I say so, that's why!" He said to the man at the door: "Shake 'em down, Andy."

Andy came over, the gun still in his hand. His hair was flaming red at the edge of his soft hat, his eyes wore a queer unfocused look. He took a gun from under Olson's coat, patted Bleyer all over in search of one, said to the pale man: "Ix-nay gun." He turned again, jammed the muzzle of the gun he still held into Bleyer's stomach so hard Bleyer bent double, said: "Where's your gun, stupid!"

Bleyer gasped: "Got none on me!" and the pale man said: "Now, Andy!" reprovingly. Then, "Look in the desk!"

Andy dug in it and found a heavy gun wrapped around in a shoulder harness and put it under his coat along with the one he had taken from Olson. He sat down on the desk with his own gun holding on the line of prisoners and the pale man said to Olson: "So lay off! You fool with this gal and it'll be just too bad."

The red-head asked: "What she want? You to find out where her old man is?" The pupils of his eyes were so wide they seemed to focus on all four against the wall at the same time.

Olson jerked his head to the side, snarled: "Ask her, you high ——!" and the red-head said: "I will, ——!" He used the same name Olson had called him, accenting it, slid off the desk over to Olson and raised the gun in his hand and slammed the muzzle into Olson's cheek. Olson had tipped his head to one side as the blow fell but the muzzle caught him on the cheek bone and he went to his knees, blood welling from a two-inch gash under his eye.

The red-head said: "Crack wise on that!"

Olson looked up at him, said: "I'll remember that and your ugly face!" The man raised the gun again and Ingrid felt Bleyer tense at her side, cry out: "No! Oley!"

The pale man said: "That's plenty, Andy! You're higher than a kite!" He didn't raise his voice but Andy let his gun drop and stood back. The pale man said: "You get the idea, boys. Just lay off." He spoke to Mrs. Kargen, said: "And you, lady, you lay off too. Just say that your old man killed the guy and leave it at that. You're giving him a break when you do." He said to the red-head: "O.K., Andy. Let's go."

The red-head said: "O.K., pal!" and the other man said: "Don't chase us out of here unless you want trouble, boys. We got guns and you ain't." He looked at Olson who was wavering to his feet, said: "I'm sorry about that!" in an apologetic voice. "Andy gets screwy when he's high."

Olson muttered something under his breath and the red-head said sharply: "What's that?"

The pale man said: "Now Andy! We'll be going!" in the same quiet voice and the red-head stopped and turned to the door and the other man followed him, backing out. He said again: "Don't follow us, boys!"

THEY HEARD the outside door slam and, with the noise, Olson jumped for the closet. He dragged out a handbag, jammed it open and took out a long-barreled pistol.

Bleyer said: "Oley! That's a twenty-two. Leave 'em go." He caught Olson by the shoulder and Olson jerked free, ran through the door into the outer room and to the hall. Bleyer reached the phone on the desk just as Ingrid screamed and he snapped out: "Quiet!"

They heard Olson call out: "Andy!" and Bleyer dropped the phone, said: "Oh God!" started toward the door. When he got to it he heard the roar of a heavy gun, then the lighter crack of the target pistol. In the second it took him to get across the outer office he heard two more heavy reports and then again the lighter gun. He got to the hall and saw Olson running down the hall toward two figures on the floor, raced after him, and saw him suddenly stop and shoot again. He came up to him as Olson stood over the two men.

The red-head was lying on his stomach with his face turned enough to show a small hole just at the side of the bridge of his nose. His eyes were open but had lost their unfocused look and were vague and blurred. Bleyer saw this, saw the pale man lying across the red-head's legs, saw the pale man jerk slightly and try to raise himself to his elbow. Olson kicked the gun from his hand, bent and lifted him by the shoulders and the man said: "Ugh! Ugh!" and choked. He tried to speak again and his throat filled with blood that gushed from his mouth and over his chin and shirt front. He slumped in Olson's arms and Olson let him down on the red-head. He looked up at Bleyer, said: "Hell! I tried to give him a break." He poked the red-head, said: "When Andy turned around and cut loose I was all set and I took him in the face. Then this guy started shooting and I popped him in the leg but he wasn't satisfied." He appealed: "You saw him start to get up."

Bleyer said: "You damn fool! Start out after two guys like that with a twenty-two target pistol."

Olson looked a little bewildered, argued: "But a little slug'll stop 'em just as well as a big one if it's put in the right place. I was all set and—" He stopped, said: "Well, see!" triumphantly and pointed to the two men on the floor.

Bleyer said: "Oh Lord!" He looked around, saw office doors opening on the hall with scared faces peering out. "Well, it might make us an ad for more business."

They heard a voice quaver: "H-h-has anybody c-c-called the p-police?" heard someone say: "Yes!" and Bleyer said to Olson: "You better go back to the office and take a good big snort and straighten out the women. I'll stay here till the law comes and bring 'em in. Tell Mrs. Kargen to tell just what happened and not to try to stall."

Olson nodded. "This is no time to make up yarns!" He stared down at the two men on the floor, then pushed through the gathering crowd and went back to the office. He frowned at Mrs. Kargen, said: "When they talk to you, just tell the truth!" And to Ingrid's excited questioning: "Never got touched. I was standing still, see, and all set. They were just turning around and couldn't connect."

Mrs. Kargen asked: "Is he dead?" and he snapped: "They're both dead!" and turned to the desk and reached in it for a bottle. He heard a bump, turned and saw Ingrid on the floor and said to Mrs. Kargen: "Get me a glass of water."

He took the bottle and held Ingrid's head from the floor, and when Mrs. Kargen handed him the water dashed it in the blond girl's face. He poured a drink into the glass and when she fluttered her eyelids and made protesting motions he held the whiskey to her lips and she drank, gagged, and sat up.

She said: "I'm all right now," then felt of her face and said: "My God! My make-up!"

Olson grinned at Mrs. Kargen who seemed entirely unexcited, said: "She's O.K. now." Still holding Ingrid close to him he reached down and poured another drink, offered it to Mrs. Kargen and, when she shook her head, drank it himself.

Ingrid said: "That water act was lousy," and started to get to her feet.

He asked: "What in the devil was the matter with you?"

She said: "You said they were both dead, didn't you? And that you weren't hit." He said: "Yes!" in a puzzled voice and she said tartly: "Well! I was thinking you were maybe shot. I was really hoping."

Olson shook his head, said: "What a girl! Us Swedes!"

She started to speak and he altered it hastily to: "I mean us Swedes and Danes!"

THERE WAS no action for three full days. A coroner's jury brought in a verdict of justifiable homicide over the death of the two men. Kowalski reported no progress in the search for Kargen. A check-up of the past of both the two men killed in the hall, and the chauffeur, revealed nothing, and the few discreet inquiries Bleyer and Olson made about Mr. and Mrs. Kargen ended in blind alleys. They were both in the office when Mrs. Kargen came in hurriedly.

She said: "I've got news!" in a hasty, excited voice, sat down and continued with, "I've heard from my husband. Just today."

Bleyer asked: "How?"

She looked suspiciously at him, said: "The police are looking for him. Will you promise not to tell."

Bleyer nodded and she said: "It was through a friend. Another flyer. A friend of Mr. Kargen's. He called me and asked me to meet him and I did and he told me he had a letter from Jack. Jack wants me to meet him."

"You going to?"

She nodded.

"Who's this friend?"

"His name is Arthur Truax. He lives at the Clinton Hotel." She hesitated, confessed: "I've never liked him. I've never thought he was as good a friend of Jack's as Jack thinks he is."

"Why that?"

"Well he—well, you know. When Jack isn't around. And then he calls me all the time when Jack is out of town."

"Whyn't you tell Jack this?"

"He'd kill him. He's got a terrible temper."

"You told us that. Do you believe this Truax now?"

"Why yes. He says Jack knows the police are looking for him and can't come and get me himself. I'm to go in the plane and meet him with Arthur."

Olson got up and walked back and forth across the office. He stopped in front of Mrs. Kargen, said: "Are you telling the truth?"

She said: "Why yes!" stiffened, got to her feet, started to speak but Olson stared at her, snapped: "If you are, somebody else ain't. This letter was to Truax, you say. Not to you?"

"Why no. Arthur read it to me."

"Then you didn't even see it. You don't know whether it was from your husband or not."

She looked troubled, said: "Why no. But then he couldn't write me. The police would get the letter and find where he was." She brightened, said: "Don't you think that's it?"

Olson said seriously: "I don't. Listen! There's been three men killed now, all of them over some deal that you don't know about. You've played ball with us and we believe you when you say you saw the chauffeur that was killed, after your husband had left. See! Where you meeting this husband of yours?"

She looked doubtful, undecided, and Olson said: "We haven't let you down yet. We'll keep it quiet. It's just protection for you."

"I'm supposed to go with Arthur and meet him about twenty miles east of a place called Trona. It's over in the desert. Jack explained where."

Bleyer said bluntly: "I think you're crazy if you go but you'll go just the same."

She smiled, said: "Yes, I will." Then, "Has anything happened?"

"Not a thing. These things take time."

"Unless you find out who did it and clear my husband we'll lose everything we've got here. We'll never be able to come back, and we own the house and some other property."

Olson said: "We'll keep at it. If worse comes to worse, he can give somebody a fake bill of sale and get his dough out when the stuff is sold." He walked to the door with her, said: "Now don't worry! Something'll break soon. You keep in touch with us, Mrs. Kargen," and went back into the office.

He mopped his forehead, said to the blond girl and Bleyer: "When she comes busting in like that, I thought sure as hell she was going to take us off the case again. She seems to have a yen for that old man of hers. Ingie, I guess you were right.

The blond girl sniffed and said: "I'm always right."

OLSON PUT his hand over the mouthpiece of the phone, said to Bleyer: "Oh God!" and to the phone: "Yes Paul... wherebouts... Clinton Hotel on East Main... I get that... Yeah!" He listened a moment more, slammed the receiver down, said: "Mrs. Kargen got stabbed to death in the Clinton Hotel. They found her about an hour ago all whittled up. Kowalski called the minute he found it out."

"They get this Truax?"

"Hell no, they've got nobody. The room was registered under some phony name. When she told us I knew it was a phony."

"Shall we call Casey and tell him about Truax?"

Olson said harshly: "Why? We're still working for her. We still got part of her dough we ain't earned. We'll get him ourselves." He jammed his hat on, snapped: "We'll pick him at the airport. If he's gone, it'll be time to tell Casey."

He slammed out of the office with Bleyer hard at his heels and the blond girl watched them leave, her face worried, and reached for the telephone.

She thought a moment, said: "I'd better not. If they should call this Casey and find I'd already done it they"—she stuck out her lower lip—"*would* raise hell."

AT THE airport, Bleyer picked the same attendant he had made friends with while waiting for Kargen, showed him his badge and a five-dollar bill, asked: "Arthur Truax. Is his plane still here?"

The man said: "Yeah, but not for long." He pointed down the runway, said: "That's it, the cabin job warming up there. The guy that's fooling around the motor is Truax."

He took the bill and Bleyer said: "Walk down that way easy with us then. We don't want him to think we want him at all."

They walked together to within fifty feet of the plane and Bleyer said: "O.K., keed, and thanks!" He jerked his head backward and the man stopped and stared after them as they walked toward the plane, looked down at the bill in his hand and shrugged his shoulders and started back.

Bleyer said: "Let's go!" slipped his gun free from the holster under his coat and, when the man by the plane turned and stared at them, snapped: "O.K., Truax. We're going to take a trip."

Truax said: "What's the idea?"

Bleyer cleared the gun, held it so the muzzle showed, said: "Get it." Truax said: "No!" and Bleyer told him: "It's either make a trip or go back to town and see whether the clerk at the Clinton recognizes you as the man that rented the room Mrs. Kargen was killed in. D'ya get that."

Truax motioned toward the cabin of the ship and Bleyer said: "You first!" and followed him in with the gun jammed against his back.

Truax said: "Where you want to go?"

Olson, following Bleyer in, said: "We won't take you out of your way. Twenty miles east of Trona to meet Kargen."

Truax asked: "You federals?"

Bleyer caught Olson's wink, said: "What do you care. Get going."

Truax settled into the control seat and Bleyer told him: "We been through that country in a car so don't make any mistakes." He grinned at Olson as the plane roared into life, said from the side of his mouth: "Just like shooting fish!"

TRONA, APPROXIMATELY one hundred and fifty miles away in an airline, took them an hour and half to reach. Ten minutes later Bleyer pushed his gun into Truax's back, shouted: "You know where to land. Don't make any mistakes." Truax shouted something back, lost some altitude and a moment later waved his hand and pointed. They started to settle and Bleyer saw Kargen's plane on the ground, saw a figure standing beside it. He pointed this out to Olson and Olson grinned, shouted: "Won't he be surprised!"

They landed a hundred yards away and Truax taxied closer until Bleyer reached past him and turned the ignition switch. He said: "End of the line!" and motioned with the gun and Truax climbed sullenly out.

As Bleyer followed him he growled: "I don't get this. Making me bring you out here!"

Bleyer grinned: "That's right, guy! Make up a story and stick to it."

Kargen's plane had the prop ticking over, with Kargen still standing at the side and a few feet from the cockpit. He saw Olson follow Truax and Bleyer from Truax's plane and started for his own ship and Olson called: "Hold tight!" and jerked his gun from under his coat. He called again: "Stay there!" and Kargen stopped and watched them come up.

He saw the gun in Bleyer's hand, looked from this to Truax, snapped out: "So I'm the goat, huh!"

Truax said: "Wait Jack! Don't fly off the handle. I couldn't…" As he spoke he came closer to Kargen and Kargen took a step forward, slammed him with his right fist and Truax went down to the sand.

Olson said: "Hold it!" and swung the gun toward Kargen.

Kargen stood back, said: "The dirty double-crossing rat!"

Truax got to his feet as Bleyer said: "He's more than that, Kargen!" and when Kargen looked away from Truax and at him, Bleyer told him: "He had a room at the Clinton Hotel. An hour before we started for here your wife was found there all cut up with a knife. Get the picture!" He stepped close to Kargen as he spoke, saw Kargen's face tighten, said: "Get it!"

Kargen said: "Dead?" and when Bleyer nodded, Kargen looked back at Truax, took a step that way.

Bleyer said: "Easy! It's all under control!"

Kargen said: "The ——!" in a choked, sick voice.

Bleyer said: "We thought maybe you got him to do it. This was one way to find out."

Kargen kept his eyes turned toward Truax and Bleyer stepped between them, said: "He'll hang for it if he did it."

Kargen said: "I guess so!" in the same odd voice.

Bleyer said: "And now, what's in that plane?"

Kargen waved his hand, said: "Make a look!"

Bleyer said: "No, you look." He waved his gun toward the cockpit, ordered: "Just unload and we'll take a look."

Kargen stepped up onto the plane and Bleyer stood to one side with Olson, watched him toss a small handbag out on the sand. Kargen straightened and Bleyer asked: "That all?"

Kargen said: "Not quite!" bent again into the cockpit and Bleyer caught the flash of light in his hand as he straightened and called harshly: "Drop it!"

He swung up his gun as Kargen turned but Kargen fired point blank at Truax when he was but half around, and, as Truax pitched forward on his face, shot again.

Olson shouted: "Drop it!"

Kargen looked down at Truax, said: "I might as well!"

Bleyer kicked the gun to one side and motioned Kargen down, turned and saw Olson on his knees by Truax.

Kargen asked: "Did I?"

Olson looked up from Truax, said: "You did!"

CASEY STARED at Olson, said: "Then you didn't really know what was going on until it was all over."

Olson explained: "Come right down to it, we don't know now. That is, everything. All we know for sure is that Kargen was running dope and aliens and what have you, and meeting Truax on the desert where they'd reship. They got away from any spotters on the other side that way. That's all we know for sure. Kargen wasn't here during the fireworks and everybody that was here is dead and can't talk. All we can do is guess."

"It sounds reasonable."

Bleyer said: "It's the only way it can be. The two guys that Oley killed with the pop gun were the distributors. Kargen's chauffeur was in it and must've jammed with them and got himself killed. Then after *they* got killed, Truax was the only one left and he figured he'd cross Kargen all the way around. I don't doubt a bit he was planning on killing Kargen when he met him out there, but of course we stopped that when we went along."

Casey said slowly: "I get all that but what about Mrs. Kargen. Why'd Truax kill her?"

"We thought first that maybe Kargen was to blame for that. We knew she was dingy about him and we thought he might be trying to get rid of her so's he could pick some other gal. See, we didn't know the dope angle until Truax cracked about whether we were federals. Kargen was just as crazy about her as she was about him though. We figure now that Truax thought she knew about the dope and might squawk. Either that or he killed her because she wouldn't run away with him. He was dingy about her himself, so my guess is the last. We'll never know."

Casey stood up, said: "He must've been crazy about her to bust Truax the way you say he did. The whole thing fits all right. I put out that Kowalski was helping me on the whole thing and we're aces now. You ought to hear Loward cry. You'd think his throat was cut." He said to Olson: "Just what in the devil is he sore at you about? He won't tell me."

"I beat him out of his place on the pistol team when I was on the force. He's never got over it."

Bleyer laughed and said: "And neither has Oley!"

They walked to the door with Casey and when he had gone, Bleyer said: "That's that. I guess we really closed that case." He said to the blonde: "And what do you think of the bosses now?"

Ingrid Jorgenson said: "What I always thought. Two muggs."

"Now Swede!"

"Dane to you!"

Olson said: "You can go home if you want. One of us'll be here if the phone rings."

She looked at her watch, said: "Three o'clock!" to herself, then, "If you're both still pinochle players and if Oley's got as much as four and a half why—" She stopped, waved her hand toward the inner room.

Bleyer nodded and Olson said: "I'm one of the best, and I have."

She jammed the cover over her typewriter and started toward the other room but stopped and turned around. She said cautiously: "Is it cash?"

ABOUT THE AUTHOR

AND HERE'S just room to introduce an author you haven't met yet, but whose stories you've been enjoying for several issues. We give you—R.(oger) D. Torrey. He says the following is frankly deleted for the sake of the public.

Three years of high school. Canadian army at sixteen. A year in a bank. Then working in a sawmill, then keeping time and books in a logging camp. Then playing piano in a theatre. Graduated, or maybe it was going the other way, into a theatre organist and worked at this until talking pictures killed this business. This took me up and down the West Coast and as far east as Tulsa, Oklahoma, though most of the time was spent in San Francisco and Los Angeles. Ran a show on the Klamath Indian Reservation until 1930. Then many things... starving and pick and shovel and driving a truck among them. Writing since the middle of 1932.

Writing crime fiction came natural. When the music business was good, every musician got around to a lot of places and met a lot of the (lower?) element, and I used to be insane about gambling, which same habit took me to even other places that serve as a base for local color. Also have chummed around with several policemen, which has helped this slant.

The hobbies are fly fishing and pistol shooting... the aversions are fishing with heavy tackle and the kind of yarns in which the hero does impossible things with a gun.

Am Irish by descent... have just turned 33... have been married and divorced... have a weakness for blondes which I fight against, knowing I can't win... another for gambling, which I've whipped. I'm too smart to even play penny ante now, though it's taken ten years to get that way.

If that's deleted, we'd like to have the spaces filled in some time and see what kind of a guy this Torrey man really is.

Roger D. Torrey

And from the way he handled the house-game atmosphere in the opening of "Dice and No Dice" we'd like to bet it's not so damn long since he dropped some dough "inside the line." How about it?

www.ingramcontent.com/pod-product-compliance
Lightning Source LLC
Chambersburg PA
CBHW030543030726
47495CB00004B/1116